Great Expectations

WORKS BY KATHY ACKER
PUBLISHED BY GROVE PRESS

Great Expectations
Blood and Guts in High School
Don Quixote
Literal Madness
Empire of the Senseless

Great Expectations

-Kathy Acker-

Grove Press
New York

The name Grove Press and the colophon printed on the title page and outside of this book are trademarks registered in the U.S. Patent and Trademark Office and in other countries.

Published by Grove Press
a division of Wheatland Corporation
841 Broadway
New York, N.Y. 10003

Library of Congress Catalog Card Number: 83-048312
ISBN: 0-8021-3155-7

First Grove Press Edition 1983
First Evergreen Edition 1983
New Evergreen Edition 1989

Manufactured in the United States of America

This book is printed on acid-free paper.

10 9 8 7 6 5 4 3 2 1

TABLE OF CONTENTS

1. PLAGIARISM

I Recall My Childhood

My father's name being Pirrip, and my Christian name Philip, my infant tongue could make of both names nothing longer or more explicit than Peter. So I called myself Peter, and came to be called Peter.

I give Pirrip as my father's family name on the authority of his tombstone and my sister—Mrs. Joe Gargery, who married the blacksmith.

On Christmas Eve 1978 my mother committed suicide and in September of 1979 my grandmother (on my mother's side) died. Ten days ago (it is now almost Christmas 1979) Terence told my fortune with the Tarot cards. This was not so much a fortune—whatever that means—but a fairly, it seems to me, precise psychic map of the present, therefore: the future.

I asked the cards about future boyfriends. This question involved the following thoughts: Would the guy who fucked me so well in France be in love with me? Will I have a new boyfriend? As Terence told me to do, I cut the cards into four piles: earth water fire air. We found my significator, April 18th, in the water or emotion fantasy pile. We opened up this pile. The first image was a fat purring human cat surrounded by the Empress and the Queen of Pentacles. This cluster, traveling through a series of other clusters that, like mirrors, kept defining or explained the first cluster more clearly—time is an almost recurring conical—led to the final unconscious image: during Christmas the whole world is rejecting a male and a female kid who are scum by birth. To the right of the scum is the Star. To the left is the card of that craftsmanship which due to hard work succeeds.

Terence told me that despite my present good luck my basic stability my contentedness with myself alongside these images, I have the image obsession I'm scum. This powerful image depends on the image of the Empress, the image I have of my mother. Before I was born, my mother hated me because my father left her (because she got pregnant?) and because my mother wanted to remain her mother's child rather than be my mother. My image of my mother is the source of my creativity. I prefer the word consciousness. My image of my hateful mother is blocking consciousness. To obtain a different picture of my mother, I have to forgive my mother for rejecting me and committing suicide. The picture of love, found in one of the clusters, is forgiveness that transforms need into desire.

Because I am hating my mother I am separating women into virgins or whores rather than believing I can be fertile.

I have no idea how to begin to forgive someone much less my mother. I have no idea where to begin: repression's impossible because it's stupid and I'm a materialist.

I just had the following dream:

In a large New England-ish house I am standing in a very big room on the second floor in the front of the mansion. This room is totally fascinating, but as soon as I leave it, I can't go back because it disappears. Every room in this house differs from every other room.

The day after my mother committed suicide I

started to experience a frame. Within this frame time was totally circular because I was being returned to my childhood traumas totally terrifying because now these traumas are totally real: there is no buffer of memory.

There is no time; there is.

Beyond the buffers of forgetting which are our buffer to reality: there is. As the dream: there is and there is not. Call this TERROR call this TOTAL HUMAN RESPONSIBILITY. The PIG I see on the edge of the grave is the PIG me neither death nor social comment kills. This TERROR is divine because it is real and may I sink into IT.

My mother often told me: "You shouldn't care if an action is right or wrong; you should totally care if you're going to profit monetarily from it."

The helmeted bowlegged stiff-muscled soldiers trample on just-born babies swaddled in scarlet violet shawls, babies roll out of the arms of women crouched under POP's iron machine guns, a cabby shoves his fist into a goat's face, near the lake a section of the other army crosses the tracks, other soldiers in this same army leap in front of the trucks, the POP retreat up the river, a white-walled tire in front of three thorn bushes props up a male's head, the soldiers bare their chests in the shade of the mud barricades, the females lullabye kids in their tits, the sweat from the fires perfumes reinforces this stirring rocking makes their rags their skins their meat pregnant: salad oil clove henna butter indigo sulfur, at the base of this river under a shelf loaded down by burnt-out cedars barley wheat beehives graves refreshment stands garbage bags fig trees matches human-brain-splattered low-walls small-fires'-smoke-dilated orchards explode: flowers pollen grain-ears tree roots paper milk-stained cloths blood bark feathers, rising. The soldiers wake up stand up again tuck in their canvas shirttails suck in cheeks stained by tears dried by the steam from hot train rails rub their sex against the tires, the trucks go down into a dry ford mow down a few rose-bushes, the sap mixes with disemboweled teenagers' blood on their knives' metal, the soldiers' nailed boots cut down uproot nursery plants, a section of RIMA (the other army) climb onto their trucks' runningboards throw themselves on their females pull out violet rags bloody tampaxes which afterwards the females stick back in their cunts: the soldier's chest as he's raping the female crushes the baby stuck in her tits

I want: every part changes (the meaning of) every other part so there's no absolute/heroic/dictatorial/S&M meaning/part the soldier's onyx-dusted fingers touch her face orgasm makes him shoot saliva over the baby's buttery skull his formerly-erect now-softening sex rests on the shawl becomes its violet scarlet color, the trucks swallow up the RIMA soldiers, rainy winds shove the tarpaulins against their necks, they adjust their clothes, the shadows grow, their eyes gleam more and more their fingers brush their belt buckles, the wethaired-from-sweating-during-capture-at-the-edge-of-the-coals goats crouch like the rags sticking out of the cunts, a tongueless canvas-covered teenager pisses into the quart of blue enamel he's holding in his half-mutilated hand, the truck driver returns kisses the blue cross tattooed on his forehead, the teenager brings down his palm wrist where alcohol-filled veins are sticking out. These caterpillars of trucks grind down the stones the winds hurled over the train tracks, the soldiers sleep their sex rolling over their hips drips they are cattle, their truck-driver spits black a wasp sting swells up the skin under his left eye black grapes load down his pocket, an old man's white hair under-the-white-hair red burned face jumps up above the sheet metal, the driver's black saliva dries on his chin the driver's studded heel crushes as he pulls hair out the back of this head on to the sheet metal, some stones blow up

My mother is the most beautiful woman in the world. She has black hair, green eyes which turn gray or brown according to her mood or the drugs she's on at the moment, the pallor of this pink emphasizes the fullness of her lips, skin so soft the color of her cheeks is absolutely peach no abrasions no redness no white tightness. This in no way describes the delicacy of the face's bone structure. Her body is equally exquisite, but on the plump or sagging side because she doesn't do any exercise and she wears girdles. She's five feet six inches tall. She usually weighs 120 pounds even though she's always taking diet pills. Her breasts look larger and fuller than they are because they sag downwards. The nipples in them are large pale pink. In the skin around the nipples and in the tops of her legs you can easily see the varicose veins breaking through. The breast stomach and upper thigh skin is very pale white. There's lots of curly hair around her cunt.

She has a small waist hands and ankles. The main weight, the thrust, the fullness of those breasts is deceptive, is the thighs: large pock-marked flesh indicates a heavy ass extra flesh at the sides of the thighs. The flesh directly above the cunt seems paler than it has to be. So pale, it's fragile, at the edge of ugliness: the whole: the sagging but not too large breasts, the tiny waist, the huge ass are sexier MORE ABOUT PASSION than a more-tightly-muscled and fashionable body.

My mother is the person I love most. She's my sister. She plays with me. There's no one else in my world except for some kind of weird father who only partly exists part out of the shadow, and an unimportant torment I call my sister. I'm watching my mother put on her tight tawny-orange sweater. She always wears a partially lacy white bra that seems slightly dirty. As she's struggling to get into a large white panty girdle she says she doesn't like girdles. She's standing in front of her mirror and mirrored dresser. Mirrors cover every inch of all the furniture in the room except for the two double beds, my father's chair, and the TV, but they don't look sensuous. Now my mother's slipping into a tight brown wool straight skirt. She always wears tight sweaters and tight straight skirts. Her clothes are old and very glamorous. She hitches her skirt up a little and rolls on see-through stockings.

She tells me to put on my coat and white mittens because we're going outside.

Today is Christmas. Huge clean piles of snow cover the streets make the streets magical. Once we get to the park below the 59th Street Bridge I say to myself, "No foot has ever marked this snow before." My foot steps on each unmarked bit of snow. The piles are so high I can barely walk through them. I fall down laughing. My mother falls down laughing with me. My clothes especially the pants around my boots are sopping wet. I stay in this magic snow with the beautiful yellow sun beating down on me as long as I can until a voice in my head (me) or my mother says, "Now you know what this experience is, you have to leave."

My mother wants to get a strawberry soda. Today my mother's being very nice to me and I love
her simply and dearly when she's being nice to
me. We're both sitting on the round red vinyl
turnable seats around the edge of the white
counter. My mother's eating a strawberry soda
with strawberry ice cream. I see her smiling. A fat
middle-aged man thinks we're sisters. My mother
is very young and beautiful.

At camp: males string tents up along a trench
filled with muck: slush from meat refuse vomit
sparkle under arching colorless weeds, the
soldiers by beating them drive back the women
who're trying to stick their kids in the shelter of
the tents, they strike at kick punch the soldiers'
kidneys while the soldiers bend over the unfolded
tent canvas. Two males tie the animals to the
rears of the tents, a shit-filled-assed teenager
squatting over the salt-eroded weeds pants dust
covers his face his head rolls vacantly around his
shoulder his purple eye scrutinizes the montage of
tents, a brown curly-haired soldier whose cheeks
cause they're crammed full of black meat are actually touching his pock-marked earlobes
crouches down next to a little girl he touches her
nape his hand crawls under the rags around her
throat feels her tits her armpits: the little girl
closes her eyes her fingers touch the soldier's
grapejuice-smeared wrist, from the shit-heaps a
wind-gust lifts up the bits of film and sex mag
pages the soldiers tore up while they were shitting
clenched the shit burns the muscles twisted by
rape. Some soldiers leaving the fire wander
around the tents untie the tent thongs they crawl
on the sand, the linen tent flaps brush their
scabies-riddled thighs, the males the females all
phosphorescent nerves huddle around the

11

candles, no longer wanting to hear anything the teenagers chew wheat they found in the bags, the kids pick threads out of their teeth put their rags on again stick the sackcloth back over their mothers' tits lick the half-chewed flour left on their lips

My mother thinks my father is a nobody. She is despising him and lashing out at him right now she is saying while she is sitting on her white quilt-covered bed "Why don't you ever go out at night, Bud? All you do is sleep."

"Let me watch the football game, Claire. It's Sunday."

"Why don't you ever take mommy out, daddy? She never has any fun." Actually I think my mother's a bitch.

"You can't sleep all the time, Bud. It isn't good for you."

"This is my one day off, Claire. I want to watch the football game. Six days a week I work my ass off to buy you and the kids food, to keep a roof over your head. I give you everything you want"

"Daddy, you're stupid." "Daddy, you don't even know who Dostoyevsky is." "What's the matter with you, daddy?"

Daddy's drunk and he's still whining, but now he's whining nastily. He's telling my mother that he does all the work he goes to work at six in the morning and comes back after six at night (which we all know is a joke cause his job's only a sine-cure: my mother's father gave him his first break, a year ago when the business was sold, part of the deal was my father'd be kept on as 'manager' under the new owners at $50,000 a year. We all know he goes to work cause there he drinks and he doesn't hear my mother's nagging). He's telling my mother he gave her her first fur coat. My father is never aggressive. My father never beats my mother up.

The father grabs a candle, the curly brownhaired soldier his red mouth rolling around the black meat takes out his knife: his hand quickly juts the red rags over his sex his pincher his grabber the curly brownhaired soldier jerks the sleepy young girl's thighs to him, she slides over the sand till she stops at the tent opening, one soldier's mutilated forehead cause he was raping over an eagle's eggs the eagle scalped him another soldier's diseased skinpores these two soldiers gag the father, the father throws a burning candle into their hairs, the curly brownhaired soldier takes the young girl into his arms, she sleeps she purrs her open palm on her forehead to his shudder trot, the clouded moon turns his naked arm green, his panting a gurgling that indicates rape the sweat dripping off his bare strong chest wakes the young girl up, I walked into my parents' bedroom opened their bathroom door don't know why I did it, my father was standing naked over the toilet, I've never seen him naked I'm shocked, he slams the door in my face, I'm curious I see my mother naked all the time, she closely watches inside his open cause gasping mouth the black meat still stuck to his teeth the black meat still in a ball, the curly brownhaired lifts her on to her feet lay her down on the dogkennels' metal grating hugs her kisses her lips the ear hollows where the bloodstained wax causes whispers his hand unbuttons his sackcloth pulls out his member, the young girl sucks out of the curly brownhaired's cheeks the black meat eyes closed hands spread over the metal grating, excited by this cheek-to-stomach muscle motion bare-headed straw-dust flying around his legs injects the devil over her scorches, the dogs waking up at the metal gratings leap out of the kennels their chains gleam treat me like a dog drag in the shit, the curly brownhaired nibbles the young girl's gums his teeth pull at the meat fibres her tongue pushes into the cracks between her teeth, the dogs howl their chains jingle against the tar of the road their paws crush down the hardened shits, the curly brownhaired's knees imprison the young girl's thighs.

My father's lying in the hospital cause he's on his third heart attack. My mother's mother at the door of my father's room so I know my father is overhearing her is saying to my mother, "You have to say he's been a good husband to you, Claire. He never left you and he gave you everything you wanted."

"Yes."

"You don't love him."

"Yes."

I know my grandmother hates my father.

I don't side with my mother rather than my father like my sister does. I don't perceive my father. My mother is adoration hatred play. My mother is the world. My mother is my baby. My mother is exactly who she wants to be.

The whole world and consciousness revolves around my mother.

I don't have any idea what my mother's like. So no matter how my mother acts, she's a monster. Everything is a monster. I hate it. I want to run away. I want to escape the Jolly Green Giant. Any other country is beautiful as long as I don't know about it. This is the dream I have:

I'm running away from men who are trying to
damage me permanently. I love mommy. I know
she's on Dex, and when she's not on Dex she's on
Librium to counteract the Dex jitters so she acts
more extreme than usual. A second orgasm cools
her shoulders, the young girl keeps her hands
joined over the curly brownhaired's ass, the wire
grating gives way, the curly brownhaired slides
the young girl under him his pants are still around
his knees his fingernails claw the soil his breath
sucks in the young girl's cheek blows straw dust
around, the mute young girls' stomach muscles
weld to the curly-headed's abdominal muscles,
the passing wind immediately modulates the least
organic noise that's why one text must subvert
(the meaning of) another text until there's only
background music like reggae: the inextricability
of relation-textures the organic (not meaning)
recovered, stupid ugly horrible a mess pinhead
abominable vomit eyes-pop-out-always-present-
ing-disgust-always-presenting-what-people-flee-
always-wanting-to-be-lonely infect my mother
my mother, blind fingernails spit the eyes
wandering from the curly-headed, the curly-
headed's hidden balls pour open cool down on
the young girl's thigh. Under the palmtrees the
RIMAS seize and drag a fainted woman under a
tent, a flushing-forehead blond soldier burning
coals glaze his eyes his piss stops up his sperm
grasps this woman in his arms, their hands their
lips touch lick the woman's clenched face while
the blond soldier's greasy wine-stained arm supports her body, the young girl RECOVERED,

New York City is very peaceful and quiet, and
the pale gray mists are slowly rising, to show me
the world, I who have been so passive and little

here, and all beyond is so unknown and great that now I am crying. My fingers touch the concrete beneath my feet and I say, "Goodbye, oh my dear, dear friend."

We don't ever have to be ashamed of feelings of tears, for feelings are the rain upon the earth's blinding dust: our own hard egotistic hearts. I feel better after I cry: more aware of who I am, more open. I need friends very much.

Thus ends the first segment of my life. I am a person of GREAT EXPECTATIONS.

I Journey To Receive My Fortune

My lawyer Mr. Gordon duly sent me his address; and he wrote after it on the card "just outside Alexandria, and close by the taxi stand." Nevertheless, a taxi-driver, who seems to have as many jackets over his greasy winter coat as he is years old, packs me up in his taxi, hems me in by shutting the taxi doors and closing the taxi windows and locking the taxi doors, as if he's going to take me fifty miles. His getting into his driver's seat which is decorated by an old weather-stained pea-green hammercloth, moth-eaten into rags, is a work of time. It's a wonderful taxi, with six great horns outside the driver's window, and ragged things behind for I don't know how many kids to hold on by, and iron spikes below them to prevent the amateur kids from yielding to temptation.

I'm just beginning to enjoy this taxi and think how like a yard of straw it is, and yet how like a rag-shop, and to wonder why the horses' nose-bags are kept inside, when I see the taxi-driver beginning to open his door as if we're going to stop presently. And stop we presently do, in a gloomy street, at certain offices with an open door, whereon is painted "EGYPT."

We're walking along the aqueduct which supplies water to the citadel. Stray dogs sleep and walk in the sun. Carrion vultures wheel through the sky. The dogs are tearing at a donkey's left-overs, especially the head which is still completely covered in skin: the head is the least edible part of

17

the skeleton. Always birds begin with eyes; dogs like the stomach or skin around the asshole. They all move from the tenderest to the toughest.

This old woman's begging me to fuck her. Puke. I prefer boys in this heat. She's uncovering her long flat tits, they look like worms, they're hanging down to her belly-button. She's stroking them. She has a sweet smile. Her head bends to one side; lips part over her yellow teeth. Another hag catches sight of me in this courtyard, cartwheels in front of me, shows me her ass. She does this when she sees a man because she wants a man so badly. A woman dancing all over her cell is beating up her tin toilet bowl like the picture we have of a crazy person cause she's not getting affection.

Three nights now I've been chasing that creep guy I'm getting sick of not getting him I'm getting sick of getting what I don't want and not getting what I want. I saw him every night at the Palace before I wanted him. He has a very pretty blonde girlfriend he's even cuter than her so I didn't want him. One night he asked me what I do with myself when he doesn't see me. He finds it hard to talk to me cause he's very shy. Since that night I've gotten this bigger crush on him and every time I've returned to the Palace every night this week—only my crush drives me out—every night this week he's never there.

Quiet way of life here—intimate, secluded. Dazzling sun effects when one suddenly emerges from these alleys, so narrow that the roofs of the shuttered bay windows on each side touch each other.

Sometimes I think about my future . . . I don't want to leave this life and go back to the horror that is New York. What shall I do when I get back to New York? What can I do to make New York not horrible? Before it descends on me and eats me up. I'm scared out of my wits.

I'm a scaredy-cat. I run away from everything. Being allowed to laze. This' what it's about.

Not only have I shirked facing my problems. I shall die at sixty before having formed any opinion concerning myself. I made a list of human characteristics: every time I had one characteristic I had its opposite.

How did I get to being always alone?

However I worry very little about any of this: I live like a plant filling myself with sun and light with colors and fresh air. I keep eating, so to speak; the digesting will have to be done then the shitting; and the shit had better be good! That's the important thing.

The day beginning to rise—I have that smartness in my eyes that comes from being up all night. Several upperclass Greek women are walking by. A pleasant fragrance wafts out from under their veils, from the raising of their elbows when they reach up to make sure their veils are still on their heads, and from the edges of the veils themselves as they float up in the draft. In my mind's eye, I see a pink stocking and a tip of a foot in a pointed yellow slipper.

Back in New York City, the tenth floor of an apartment building on 73rd street and Third Avenue:
HUBBIE: Goodbye, dear. (Shouting) I'm going to Long Island to go hunting.

WIFE (entering their wall-to-wall carpeted living room): But you can't leave me. It's Christmas.

HUBBIE: This is my vacation. I worked like a dog all year to keep you in trinkets and furs. I want to do what I want for once in my life and it's Christmas.

WIFE: You're gonna desert us on Christmas! You louse! You lousy louse! Mother always said you were a louse and, besides, she has more money than you! I don't know why I married you I certainly didn't marry you for your money. (Starts to sob)

HUBBIE: Stop it, dear. (Doesn't know what to do when he sees a woman crying. It makes him feel so helpless.) The children'll see and think something's the matter.

WIFE: We don't have any children. It's all your fault.

HUBBIE: It's always my fault. Everything's always my fault. When your dog died when you were four years old it was my fault. When Three Mile Island was leaking away Mother threw out her new General Electric microwave cause she said it was a UFO Martian breeding ground: I caused that one. Your commie actor friends're always telling me I'm not political enough cause I won't stand on streetcorners and look like a bum just to hand out that rag (SEMIOTEXT(e)) they call a newspaper a bum wouldn't even use to wipe his ass with, some communism, and then they say I'm responsible for the general state of affairs. All I do is work every day! I never say anything about anything! I do exactly what every other American middle-aged man does. Everything's my fault.

WIFE (soberly): Everything IS your fault. (The wife starts to cry again.)

You don't love me enough. You don't want me to be a little girl. I'm . . . mmwah (her hands crawl at one of the lapels of his red-and-black hunting jacket). I'm a . . . googoo. Don't you love me? Bobby? Do you love me and be nice to me and don't desert me cause I love you so much?

HUBBIE (completely bewildered): Of course I love you. (His big strong arms pick her up. He carries her into the bedroom. He puts his cock into her pink rayon panties. He comes. He wants to do what he wants to do.)

WIFE: You promised and you can't break your promise you'd stay here.

HUBBIE: Shit. (He fondles his old Winchester. He walks over to one of the large living room windows and sticks the rifle through the window. He shoots down a streetlight that's red.) Goddamn.

WIFE: Bobby, what're you doing? Don't you know we all—the tenants—decided we'd have noise regulations during the night?

HUBBIE: I can have my shooting practice right here. Bam bam (says as he shoots). Three dead streetlights. Try crossing the street now, President Carter.

WIFE: Don't insult President Carter that way.

HUBBIE: Bam. (The bullet goes right through a businessman's hat. The businessman doesn't notice a thing.) Bam bam bam bam. (The lamps which light the street below Mary and Bobby's apartment burst open.) Those local hoods can thank me: tonight they'll jerk their girlfriends off in the doorways and the cops won't see a thing.

WIFE: You're acting just like Mother said you would when you don't get your way. All you want is attention. You're gonna be a baby until I give in to you. Well, I'm not going to. I've got myself to think about.

HUBBIE: Bam. (Shoots down a four-year-old girl who's wearing a baby-blue jumper. Her junked-out mother is too shocked to scream. It begins to snow.) Guess it's gonna snow for Christmas.

WIFE: Ooh, I'm so glad! Now aren't you glad you stayed home for Christmas?

Scene 2. The Husband's Monológue.

WIFE: Where're you going, Frank?

HUBBIE (putting on a torn khaki jacket over his checkered hunting jacket): I'm just going out for a second, hon. There're a few things I can't reach from here.

WIFE (flinging her arms across the door like she's Jesus on the cross): You're not going out on this cold night. Something horrible's gonna happen.

HUBBIE (shouldering his gun): Don't be ridiculous, Mary. There's nothing out there.

WIFE: You're going to get drunk and hang around with loose women and God knows what and Josie and Ermine're coming at seven!

HUBBIE: Aw, honey. I don't want to see those alcoholics.

WIFE: Josie and Ermine aren't alcoholics. Ermine earns $75,000 a year.

HUBBIE: They drink up all my Scotch. I'll tell you what. If they come in here, I'll go bang-bang and Winchester will get rid of the beggars. I told you I was getting you a nice Christmas.

WIFE: You'll do your shooting on the street. I just washed the kitchen floor.

22

HUBBIE: Here we go round the mulberry bush the mulberry bush the mulberry bush . . . I'm a child again. I'm happy. I haven't been happy since I went out drinking with that black whore who threatened to burn my balls off with her BIC just cause I was teasing her a little about her kid sister. Women are too sensitive. Take my wife. Premonitions! (Huge black shadows start gathering around the husband.) Boy did she get hot under the collar huh . . . about nothing . . . about a dead four-year-old who in two years would be hooked on junk. All women are hooked on junk. Now I can do whatever I want.

Is there anything else? Is there anything else? What is it to know?

I, Peter, don't know because I obsessively adore my father. My father was a poor German-Jewish refugee. He came to America and started a successful millinery business in those old days when men weren't allowed to have their own businesses. Then he married a rich woman, well that's what men did in those days, that's the only way they could succeed. That and being pimps. Women don't realize that marriage is a business for men—clothes makeup all the stuff women belittle; they want the men to wear that stuff and then they say "Men's stuff is unimportant;" marriage and sex are the only business men got. My father thought money was everything; he had a right to think money was everything; he didn't have a choice of thinking anything else considering where he lived when and he had made himself a success.

Unfortunately I'm shit to him because I don't want to earn money. I don't know what to do because I honor him and what he's done.

My mother is a dummy and a piece of jellyfish. The most disgusting thing in this world is her. My worst nightmare is that I'll have some of that jellyfish in me.

My mother, the jellyfish, wants me to be just like I am.

So I fall down in a fit. I decide to be totally catatonic. I am unable to know anything. I have no human contacts. I'm not able to understand language.

They call me CRAZY. But I'm not inhuman. I still have burning sexual desires. I still have a cock. I just don't believe there's any possibility of me communicating to someone in this world.

I hate humans who want me to act like I can communicate to them. I hate feeling more pain because I've felt so much pain.

My idea of happiness is numbness.

From what I've seen and read I think the people who live in Egypt don't absolutely hate their lives.

I feel I feel I feel I have no language, any emotion for me is a prison

I think talking to humans, acting in this world, and hurting other humans are magical acts. I fall in love with the humans who I see do these things

I think these categories: this logic way of talking (perceiving) is wrong.

THERE'S NO SUCH THING AS POWER AND POWERLESSNESS. For instance, I, Peter, am totally passive or powerless. I live in a world in which one major power, the USA, is trying to artificially create a war with another great power to increase its military budget. All rich businessmen get richer while wars are always fought on top of the bodies of poor people. We are really really powerless.

Anything mental is real.

Dear Peter,
          I think your new girlfriend stinks. She is a liar all the way around because her skin is yellow from jaundice, not from being Chinese like she pretends. She's only pretty because she's wearing a mask. You're hooked on her tight little cunt: it's only a sexual attraction I know you're very attracted to sex cause when you were young you were fat and no girl wanted to fuck you. What you don't know is that this cunt contains lots of poisons—not just jaundice—a thousand times more powerful than the coke she is feeding you to keep you with her—especially one lethal poison developed by the notorious Fu Manchu that takes cocks, turns their upper halves purple, their lower parts bright red, the eyes go blind so they can no longer see what's happening, the person dies. Your new girlfriend is insane and she's poisoning you.
                    Love,
                         Rosa

P.S. I'm only telling you this for your own good.

Dear Peter,

        I want you wet. I want you dripping all over me. I want you just for sex. Once I know I can have you I might ignore you I know that would be very stupid. Then you'd run away as fast as you could. Then I'd want you so much I'd figure more subtle lasting ways to commit suicide than all the ways—like lobotomy, everyone in my family goes, I robot flesh made of steel—I have these past two years since you left me. Ours is the hottest love affair that has ever existed and I'm telling everyone that it is so. Physical sex doesn't have to have anything to do with love affairs. Love affairs are when each person can do anything they want and the other person realizes that the most unbelievable behavior possible is usual.

        Love,

           Rosa

The Gritty State Of Things To Come

Dear Sylvére,

        This serves you right. I told you this was going to happen. Now that I've spent last night fucking you, I'm in love with you. I'm writing these few lines to give you the news and the news isn't good. A few minutes ago the cops arrested me for stealing a copy of SEMIOTEXT(e). You keep talking about how you're making Italian terrorism fashionable: isn't my ass here in New York worth at least a penny to you for every dollar of Italian terrorist ass over there? I think you should be nice to me because I'm just a helpless little girl. Also please try to get permission to come to see me and bring me some underwear. Put in your cat because I need affection and you don't need anything. How are you? Darling, I'm awfully sorry about what's happening to me. Let's face it: some kids are born with silver spoons in their mouths. I'm an old woman whose teeth are falling out. I'm counting on you to help me out. I wish I could run into your chest and climb on your arms three hours a week and no more. Remember what we do together when I'm unparanoid enough to see you. Remember what we do together when I'm unparanoid enough to see you. Try to recognize the only reality of the real world: no one gives a shit about anything. Get on your knees, sweetheart, and kiss the earth,

Love,
Rosa

We Have Proven That Communication Is Impossible

Dear Susan Sontag,
            Would you please read my books and make me famous? Actually I don't want to be famous because then all these people who are very boring will stop me on the street and bother me already I hate the people who call me on the phone because I'm always having delusions. I now see my delusions are more interesting than anything that can happen to me in New York. Despite everyone saying New York is just the most fascinating city in the world. Except when Sylvère fucks me. I wish I knew how to speak English. Dear Susan Sontag, will you teach me how to speak English? For free, because, you understand, I'm an artist and artists by definition are people who never pay for anything even

though they sell their shows out at $10,000 a painting before the show opens. All my artist friends were starving to death before they landed in their middle-class mothers' wombs; they especially tell people how they're starving to death when they order $2.50 each beers at the Mudd Club. Poverty is one of the most repulsive aspects of human reality: more disgusting than all the artists who're claiming they're total scum are the half-artists the hypocrites the ACADEMICS who think it's in to be poor, WHO WANT TO BE POOR, who despise the white silk napkins I got off my dead grandmother—she finally did something for me for once in her life (death)—because those CRITICS don't know what it's like to have to tell men they're wonderful for money, cause you've got to have money, for ten years. I hope this society goes to hell. I understand you're very literate, Susan Sontag,

      Yours,

             Rosa

Dear David,

      Are you a Tibetan monk yet? I used to hate you because you didn't love me so much you would give up your whole life for me. I expect this of every man. In retrospect, I realize that I was also selfish: I should have stopped making demands that you not be the closet female-hating sadist you are. I understand it's very hard to be rich because rich people are trained, they can't just be poor, they are trained to act as if they need to work and be big worldly successes. Your explanation that you gave up writing your visions in order to do commercial Hollywood script writing because you needed Francis Ford Coppola's

$150,000 when you receive huge monthly estate checks rivals a university professor's essay on the similarities between *Moby Dick* and Nazism. At least a university professor really has to make a living. (Language means nothing anymore ✳ anyway.)Walking down Second Avenue with you while you're telling me you're as poor as me when I know I have to fuck thirteen-inchers in porn films the next day so I can pay Peter, my husband, his goddam rent wasn't as bad as how my other boyfriends treated me: at least you bought me lunch at Amy's after we fucked. The only thing I resent is when you were doing everything you could to force me to fuck your Tibetan guru and I had bad gonorrhea. That your environmental richness does not excuse.

I'd like to fuck you when you return from London,

      Yours,
         Rosa

Dear Steve Maas,

        Why don't you give some of the money you are making off the Mudd Club to the poor starving artists who're supporting it? Diego says you're a millionaire now. Michael Betsy many of my friends, you know who they are, are desperate. You're always saying you want to do something for art and you understand what art is. If you understand what art is, you wouldn't be a power-monger: you'd let artists have the door at least between twelve and two, not between nine and eleven—as it is now—before anyone's even allowed in the club.

      Yours,
         Rosa

Dear God,

I used to complain that the world isn't fair. Now I don't think the world isn't fair. I don't think. Have you made me into a lobotomy case? Has the world turned me into a lobotomy case? You are the world. I wish there was a man here who could put me back in touch with the world,

Love,
Rosa

"You'll be a friend to me, won't you?"

"I'll try. But you know, it's not easy to be your friend."

"It isn't? Why?"

"Oh, I'm such a mite of a thing and you're so gorgeous. You always know what you're doing. You're so sure of yourself you could crush me. You make me feel like I'm nothing, I know you don't mean it."

"No one loves me, I lead this horrible life. Don't think I'm someone I'm not. I'm like a hermit a nothing, I think I'm one of the true innocents."

"You not being hermetic with me. You're open and friendly!" Rosa, the pupil in the Nuns' House says.

"How can I help it, sweetie? You fascinate me."

"Me?" Rosa half-questions and, half-teasing, pretends to question. "It's too bad Peter doesn't feel it."

The girls in the Nuns' House heard endlessly every detail of Peter's and Rosa's relations.

"Peter adores you!" O, the orphan who's the new pupil exclaims, fiercely blazing if Peter doesn't adore Rosa she'll make him do it.

"Well . . . he likes me," Rosa begins to own up, twists her fingers in each other there's still a bit of a question, "I know he does. Our arguments are my fault. My mind won't stay still. I'm never contented. Everything dissatisfies me. Still . . . he CAN be ridiculous!"

O's eyes demand what can possibly be ridiculous about gentle Peter. These days none of the boys are gentle.

"He never buys me coffee (Rosa means 'he never buys me expensive meals') . . . and he manipulates me I know he's manipulating me he's waving things over my head like marriage he knows I want to get married and he's using my want to control me even though he's a wimp." Rosa answers as if everything she's saying is absolutely true.

O's realizing in a world where affection's possible she will have none. Consciousness of this pain gives her power. She without thinking grabs Rosa's hands and says, "Please, be my friend. I need affection."

"I'll be your friend," Rosa replies straightway, "though you're so far above me you must have lots of friends. I'll be true to you and if I ever let you down, please understand, I don't mean to let you down, I'm just weak. I don't know anything about myself. You help me find who I am. You talk straight to me."

O hugs her friends and holds her in her arms. "Tell me, Rosa. Who is this Mr. Sadat?"

Rosa shakes. Her eye pupils look slightly upwards.

"Just before I came here, my brother and I met him."

"He's Peter's uncle."

"You don't like him?"

"Oh!" Rosa's hands go over her face. "No."

"He says he loves you very much."

"Oh." Rosa hugs her new resource (friend) even closer. "I don't want to know . . . I don't know what there is about him that makes me feel this way. It doesn't make sense. I'm scared of him beyond any reason I know of. I think about him all the time. He terrifies me. He can get at me even when he's not around. He's evil. There's no such thing as evil."

"What happened between you and him?"

"I can't talk now. I'm sorry. In a minute. Please don't go away from me. I'll be able to talk in a minute."

"He DID do something horrible, didn't he?"

"No . . . no. He's very kind. He acts as he should. He never SAYS anything."

"And yet . . . ?"

"He doesn't say anything, but I know, I know it's true. He wants to have power over me he almost has power over me, I can hardly fight. He always acts kind to me. I have no reason to think this. I can't tell it to anyone. I'm mad. When I'm playing piano, his eyes are always on my hands. When I'm singing I'm a horrible singer, his eyes are always on my lips. He's telling me he's controlling me I'm accepting that I'm accepting our nonverbal agreement. I don't look at him. That doesn't matter. Every now and then my eyes have to brush by his our eyes meet just for a second, this means I agree I'm under his spell. Sometimes he's so powerful but he's not there, do you know what I mean, he's like a robot. I don't have any way of talking to him."

"What could he actually want from you?"

"I don't know. All I do is fear. I can't see beyond fear."

"Did anything else happen tonight?"

"No. Tonight his look was more compelling . . . his eyes stood on me more unmovingly than they ever have. He was holding me in his arms tonight. I couldn't bear the darkness. I cried out. Don't tell this to anyone. It's not true. Whatever you do don't tell Peter, please don't mention a word to Peter because he's Peter's uncle. Tonight you said you're strong, you don't know what fear is, please please be strong for me. I used to not know what fear is. I used to have the strength to believe what I feel is real and my affection for people makes me human. I can talk to you. You can't go away. Don't reject me. I'm scared now that I'm asking you you'll walk away."

The lustrous gypsy-face droops over those clinging arms and chest; the wild black hair falls over the thin form. The intense eyes hold a sleeping burning energy, now softened by compassion and wonder. Let the man who's concerned NOTICE this!

Mr. Anwar Sadat's monologue:

I'm seeing everything I've ever done rise up before me, just as they are; I have to see (face) everything, nothing is left untouched. I must see everything face-to-face, every action I do, and only finally when that is over, when I'm no longer horror, will I be free.

War is coming. I hate to say it, but it is. A more devastating war than before and the end of the world as we now know this world. There will be no more money, not much food or heat, diseases rampage, and fear hallucination will reign. It will be the days of nothing and the days of a kind of plenty where there are no causes and effects.

There's no way to prepare for horror. Language like everything else will bear no relations to anything else. The business corporations who'll run the war are now bringing triple amounts of heroin and coke into this country to prepare the citizenship for soldiery. "Another?" says this woman, in a querulous rattling whisper. "Have another?"

The Lascar dribbles at the mouth. The graves are still.

"What visions can SHE have? Visions of more butcher shops and bars and MasterCharge cards? More and more people dying to throw their useless money away eat eat this horrible bed without these bodies on it this wall smooth and sanitary? What relations can drugged-up people have?"

He listens to the mutterings.

"Unintelligible!"

Culture has been chattering and chattering but to no purpose. When a sentence becomes distinct, it makes no more sense or connection. Wherefore the watcher says again "Unintelligible," nods his head, and smiles gloomily. He puts a few coins on the table, grabs a cap, gropes his way down the broken stairs, mumbles good-morning to some rat-ridden super sitting in an old plastic chair under the stairs, and passes out.

Dear Peter,

        I'm finding it very hard to live without you.

The whole day long, in that rather too coun- trified house at Tansonville, which had the air merely of a place to rest in when out for a stroll or during a shower, one of those houses in which

34

every drawing-room gives the effect of a summerhouse, and where, in the bedrooms, on the wallpaper of one of the roses of the garden, and on the wallpaper of the other birds from the trees have come to join you and keep you company (but one by one, at any rate, for these are old-fashioned wallpapers, on which each rose is so distinct it could have been picked if it had been real, and each bird could be put in a cage and tamed) having none of the pretentious interior decorating of the rooms of this day, in which, on a silver background, all of apple trees of Normandy stand out sharply in Japanese style, to fill with fantasies these hours spent closeted up—that whole day I remained in my room, which looked out on the beautiful verdure of the estate and the lilacs at the entrance border, on the tall trees at the edge of the water, their green foliage glistening in the sunlight, and on the forest of Meseglise. The only reason, at bottom, why I enjoyed looking at Proust's words was because I said to myself, "It's pleasant to have so much verdure at my bedroom window," until suddenly, in the vast, verdant picture I recognized—but brushed by contrast in deep blue simply because it was farther away—the spire of the church at Combray, not a representation of that spire, but the spire itself, which, bringing thus before my eyes distance in both space and time, had come and outlined itself on my windowpane in the midst of the given foliage but in a very different tone, so dark that it almost seemed as if it had been merely sketched in. And, if I stepped out of my room for a moment, at the end of the hall, because the hall faced in a different direction, I caught sight of a band of scarlet, as it were, just the wall covering of a small drawing-room which

35

was of simple mousseline, but red and quick to burst into flame if a ray of sun was falling on it.

During our walks together, Gilberte talked to me about the way Robert was losing interest in her and increasing his attentions to other women. And it is true that his life was cluttered up with many affairs with women which, like certain masculine friendships in the lives of men who prefer women, had an air of hopelessly trying to defend their position and uselessly taking up space which, in most houses, characterizes objects that can serve no useful purpose.

During our many walks together, Peter's new girlfriend Shang-shi talked to me about the way Peter was losing interest in her and increasing his attentions to other women. And it is true that his life was cluttered up with many affairs with women which, like certain masculine friendships in the lives of men who prefer women, had an air of hopelessly trying to defend their position and uselessly taking up space which, in most houses, characterises objects that can serve no useful purpose.

"How much?" I ask the taxi-driver.

The taxi-driver answers, "A dollar—unless you wish to make it more."

I naturally say I have no wish to make it more.

"Then it must be a dollar," observes the taxi-driver. "I don't want to get into trouble. I know HIM!" He blackly closes an eye at my lawyer Mr. Gordon's name and shakes his head.

Anwar Sadat climbs up a broken staircase, opens the door in front of him, looks into a dark stifling room, and says, "Are you alone now?"

"I'm always alone. Worse luck for me, deary, and better for you," a croak replies. "Come in, come in, whoever you are: I can't see you 'til I light this match, I recognize your voice I think. I know you, don't I?"

"Light that match and see."

"Oh oh deary I will oh oh, my hand is shaking so I can't put it on a match all of a sudden. And I cough so (cough cough) everytime I put these matches down they jump around, I never know where they are. Oh oh oh. They're jumping around, this damn cough, like living things. Are you planning to go somewhere, deary?"

"No."

"Not planning to go on a long trip?"

"No way."

"Well, there are people who travel by land and people who travel by sea. I'm the mother of both. I provide men with everything. Not like that Jack Chinaman Ludlow Street. He don't know what it is to father farther and mother. He don't know how to cut this, he charges what I charge and more, much much more, whatever he'll get. Here's a match, sweetie, uh-oh. Where's that candle? I never could stand electric lights. Everytime I start to cough, I cough out twenty of those damn matches before I get one lit. (She manages to light a match before she starts heaving again.) My lungs are gone! (Yellow phlegm) Oh oh oh!'' While she's grabbing for her breath she can't see, all of her senses are dead, except the senses of coughing; now it's over—eyes open— life returning, "Oh, you."

"You're surprised to see me?"

"Aren't you dead?"

"Why do you think I'm dead?"

"You've been away from me for so long. How can you stay alive for three hours without me? Something bad must have happened to you?"

"Not at all. A relative died."

"Died of what, deary?"

"Probably, death."

Beginning her process and starting to bubble and blow at the faint spark enclosed in the hollow of her hands, she speaks from time to time, in a tone of snuffling satisfaction, without leaving off.

WHERE DO EMOTIONS COME FROM, ARE EMOTIONS NECESSARY, WHAT DO EMO- TIONS TELL US ABOUT CONSCIOUSNESS?

She gives the man her brown leather bag.

She is sitting next to a man and her ass is bare on the taxicab fake leather.

He is reaching down into her blouse and mak- ing her pull off her clothes.

He's leaving her alone and she doesn't know how to handle an alien world.

He takes her somewhere she's never been before.

38

His hands are touching her sweater.

His hands are lifting her sweater up her back.

His hands are running down the outward slope of her ass.

His right hand's third finger is sitting in her asshole and his right hand thumb is an inch in her cunt.

He makes her cry out sharply.

His right hand is pushing her down.

His hard cock sticks into her hole.

He thrusts into her asshole without using any lubrication.

His knees stick into her face.

He explains to her she's not going to know.

His strong arm pulling on her arms is lifting her to her feet.

He shows her his whip.

One of his hands lies on her left shoulder.

He tells her she can expect he will hurt her mentally and physically.

He hurts her physically to give her an example.

He tells her there are no commitments and she

has to let him make all the decisions, she won't make any more decisions.

IS THERE ANY NEED FOR EMOTION?

He says to her, "Nothing you have, even your mind, is yours anymore. I'm a generous man. I'm going to give you nothing."

She's turning around and catching his eyes staring at her as if he loves her.

She is sitting next to him and listening to him talk.

He is saying that it no longer matters what she thinks and what her choices are.

He is saying that he is the perfect mirror of her real desire and she is making him that way.

His eyes are not daring to meet her eyes.

He is walking back and down and in front of her.

He is dialing her phone number on the phone.

He's telling her to wait without any clothes on for him to come over.

He's telling her to throw out certain identities and clothes he doesn't like.

He's telling her he doesn't have any likes or dislikes so there's no way she can touch him.

40

He's telling her he's a dead man.

She's laying out her clothes and wondering which one's the softest.

She's wondering if she's going to die.

She is waiting for this man who says he's not her lover by trying to guess what he wants.

He is telling her iron becomes her.

He is seizing her by the throat and hair.

She is thinking that it is not a question of giving her consent and it is never a question of choice.

So what use is emotion? What use is anything? Oh, oh, she isn't understanding.

NOT ONLY IS THERE NO ESCAPE FROM PERCEIVING BUT THE ONLY WAY TO DEAL WITH PAIN IS TO KILL ONESELF TOTALLY BY ONESELF. SUICIDE HAS ALWAYS BEEN THE MOST DIFFICULT OF HUMANITY'S PROBLEMS.

Caress the tips of your nipples.

I'm giving you away so you have no choice who your teacher is.

Take off your skirt.

Suck me.

You don't care who you fuck.

Sex is only physical.

Play with your clit.

You'll obey me without loving me.

When you arrive, your eyes show happiness.

My hands are rubbing your breasts.

My lips are touching your breasts.

My lips are your lips.

When will you bring your whip?

I'm doing everything I can to understand.

I'm doing everything I can to control.

I'm doing everything I can to love (name).

My consciousness is letting loose every kind of emotion.

You will masturbate in front of me.

You are a whore.

All women are whores.

BLOOD SEEPS OUT OF ONE OF THE GIRLS' CUNTS WHILE HER LEGS ARE SPREAD OPEN

Hatless, wearing practically no makeup, her hair totally free, she looks like a well-brought-up little girl, dressed as she is in a very full wool

42

tweed little boys' trousers and a box-cut matching jacket, or little hand-knit pale blue or red sweaters, tiny collars around the neck, flopping over full-cut velvet trousers, pale blue silk slippers tied around her ankles, or her evening narrow black knee-length dress. Everywhere Sir S takes her people think she's his daughter and her addressing him in the most formal terms while he acts familiarly with her underlines this mistake. Sitting in an all-night restaurant during the early morning hours before gray light starts to appear walking past the few trees that exist at the lower end of Fifth Avenue while the evening sky is unable to turn completely black, an old woman in the restaurant begins to talk to them the people on the street smile at them.

Once in a while he stops next to a concrete building and puts his arms around her and kisses her and tells her he loves her. THE FUTURE: once he invites her to lunch with two of his Italian compatriots. This is the first time he's invited her to meet any of his friends. Then he shows up an hour before he said he was going to.

He has the keys to her place. She's naked. She's just finished meditating. She realizes he's carrying what looks like a golf club bag. He tells her to open his bag.

The whips are pink silk and pale black fur and one plaster and leather with tiny double and triple knots so there're no expectations and dolls and a long light brown whip that looks like the tail of a thin animal.

The minute he touches her she begins to come.

For the first time he asks her what her taste is.

She can't answer.

He tells her she's going to help him destroy her. Whips don't exist and are ridiculous. Who could confuse orgasm with pain?

The three girls, in the school bathroom cold tiled floor, are giggling.

It's the first time he's taken her out and not treated her like a piece of shit.

The Swords Point Upwards

The man and the woman are sitting in the first restaurant he's ever taken her to. One of the man's friends is sitting in an armchair to her right, another to her left. The one on the left is tall, red-haired, gray-eyed, 25 years old. The man is telling his two friends he invited them to have dinner with the woman so they could do whatever they want with her in no uncertain terms because she's the most unnameable unthinkable spit spit. She realizes that she is at the same time a little girl absolutely pure nothing wrong just what she wants, and this unnameable dirt this thing. This is not a possible situation. This identity doesn't exist.

Her grandmother lifts up her pink organdy skirt to show the hotel headwaiter, "Look what my granddaughter's wearing! Her first new girdle! And only six years old!"

The first man doesn't recognize her humanity. All the men she has don't recognize her humanity. Kneel down suck off our cocks. While you're sucking them off, use the fingers of both hands with those quick feather ways you do. Then they all go away as quickly as possible while she's swallowing their cum.

The young boys being completely overwhelmed by her strength—her calm existing in such contradiction—tell her they want her to tell them everything. They give themselves over to her as if

44

they're clay, not human. They fuck again and again. They can't get enough fucking. Then they turn on her. They hate her guts because she allowed them to be weak. They want to beat her up.

The following day, scared she'll leave him, he tells her the red-haired boy says he wants to marry her and so take her away from this unbearable contradiction in which she's living.

It's always her decision. She tells him she wants to become another, as if at this point it's even a question of a decision, though it always is.

Animality

Sparrow-hawk, falcon, owl, fox, lion, bull: nothing but animal masks, but scaled to the size of the human head, made of real fur and feathers, the eye crowned with lashes when the actual animal has lashes, as the lion has, and with pelts and feathers falling to the person-wearing-them's shoulders. A molded, hardened cardboard frame placed between the outer facing and the skins' inner lining keep the mask shape rigid. The most striking and the one she thinks transforms her the most is the owl mask because tan and tawny fathers whose colors are her cunt hairs make it; the feathery cape almost totally hides her shoulders, descending halfway down the back, and the front to the beginning of the breasts' swell.

"But O, and I hope you'll forgive me, you'll be taken on a leash."

Natalie returns holding the chain and pliers which Sir S uses to force open the last link. He fastens it to the second link of the chain stuck in her cunt. After she remasks herself, Sir S tells Natalie to take hold of the end of the chain and

45

walk around the room, ahead of her. (being chained to the text)

"Well I must say," he remarks, "the Commander's right, all the hair'll have to be removed. Meanwhile keep wearing your chain."

What shocks and upsets the girl at the depilatory parlor the following day, more than the irons and the black-and-blue marks on her lower back, are the brand new whip marks. No matter how many times she repeats attempts to explain, if not what her fate (decision) is, at least that she's happy; there's no way of reassuring this girl or allaying her feelings of disgust and terror. No matter how much she thanks these people how polite just like a little girl she acts when she's leaving this parlor where for hours she's lain her legs spread as wide as possible not to get fucked but to get love, it doesn't matter how much money she gives all of them; she feels they're rejecting her rather than her walking out of a business appointment. She realizes that there's something shocking in the contrast between the fur on her belly and the feathers on her mask just as she realizes that this air of an Egyptian statue which the mask lends her, and which her broad shoulder narrow waist and muscled legs serve only to emphasize, demands her flesh be absolutely hairless.

Stared at them with eyes opened wide, deaf to human language and dumb. People seeing her, with expressions of horror and contempt turn and flee. Sir S is using O model to demonstrate. Stone wax unhuman. Daybreak is awakening the asleep. Unfasten chains, remove masks.

The Beginning

As you and Sir S are walking out of the subway station, up to the street, a young cop or a young man who looks like a cop, as soon as he sees Sir S, steps forward from a large black Mercedes whose doors are locked. He bows, opens the rear car door, and steps aside. After you've settled in the back seat, your luggage in the front seat, Sir S' lips lightly brush your right cheek and he closes the door.

The car starts suddenly, so fast you don't know enough to grab him to call out. Although you throw yourself against the moving back window, he's gone forever you feel frenzy.

The car is rapidly moving westward into the countryside. You are oblivious to the outside world because you are crying.

The terrorist driver is tilting his seat so it's almost horizontal to pull your legs on to the front seat. Your legs are pressing the ceiling as he's plunging his huge cock into you. He doesn't stop for an hour. He moans loudly when he comes.

The driver is 25 years old. He has a thin narrow face, large black eyes. He looks very sensitive and at the edge of being weak. His mouth never approaches your mouth. There is a basic agreement that the act of kissing is far more explosive than that of fucking.

When he finishes fucking you, you pull down your skirt and then button your thin hand-crocheted linen sweater through whose lace delicate puckers of nipples can be seen. You carefully place red lipstick over your lips.

If you want to, you can reach out and grab armfuls of red foxgloves.

"The driver raped you. You're two hours late.

contradiction

You let him rape you."

"Everything happens as Sir S says. Is he going to come?"

"I think so. I don't know when."

The tenseness felt in all your muscles when you're asking this question slowly dissolves and you look at this woman gratefully: how lovely she is, how sparkling with her hair streaked with gray. She's wearing over black pants and a matching blouse, an antique Chinese jacket.

Obviously the rules which govern the dress and conduct of the terrorists don't apply to her.

"Today I want to have lunch with you. Go wash yourself. At 3 o'clock sharp I'll be back."

You silently follow her; you're floating on cloud nine: Sir S says he'll see you again.

In this female terrorist house which is disguised as a girls' school, you're free to move around. You're standing on the Delancey Street corner. It's raining lightly. You know you're older than the other girls. (A man might not want you cause the skin on your face's slightly wrinkled. Men want young tight fresh girl skin. They want new. They want to own. They want to be amazed.) You're gonna have to work three times as hard as the other girls to get your men. This work is creating an image which men will strongly crave. This image has to be composed (partly) of your strong points and has to picture something some men beyond rationality want. You have to keep up this image to survive.

You put all thoughts away. Thoughts can be present in those hiatuses when you're not a machine moving to survive. You are a perfect whore so you're not human.

Get off this. "Hi honey, I can do anything."

Your hips wiggle far wider than any other whore's hips. You're stealing outright from the restaurants you're sitting in you're laughing in those faces of big businessmen who look like pigs when a bum's pulling a knife on you you say, "Honey, it's too short." Nothing can touch (hurt) you when you're moving this fast: a perfect image: closed.

This' why you're the best whore in the world. You have to make this image harder. While you're a whore, you can love someone. While you're a whore, it's impossible for anyone to love you.

Sir S wants you to prostitute to bring him money.

"Listen, O, I've heard quite enough. If Sir S wants you to go to bed for money, he's certainly free to do so. It's not your concern. Go to sleep now, baby, shut up. As for your other duties and obligations, we use the sister system here. Noelle will be your sister, and she'll explain all the procedures to you."

The whores spend most of their time with other whores and live in a steamy, hot atmosphere, a dressing room (perhaps one pimp who is a cardboard figure over whom they obsess just like the pupils in an all-girls' school and the one male religion teacher), here at the edge of being touchable. Their knowledge of how vulnerable each of them is defines their ways of talking to each other and creates a bond, the strongest interfemale bond women know, between them.

Women's sexuality isn't goal-oriented, is all-over. Women will do anything, not for sex, but for love, because sex isn't a thing to them, it's all over undefined, every movement motion to them is a sexual oh. This is why women can be sexually honest and faithful. This is why women look up to things, are amazed by things. Women hate things the most.

Running the tip of his riding crop over the skin of your breasts.

"Why didn't you bring your whips tonight? At least you can slap my face."

Takes hold of your large nipples and pulls.

Calls you "a whore."

You're tightening around the flesh pole that fills and burns you. The pole doesn't move out.

"Caress me with your mouth."

You enjoy prostituting with this stranger.

She kisses the tip of one of your breasts through the black lacework covering it.

"They won't tell me their names," she says. "But they look nice, don't they?"

The men are embarrassed and vulgar. Their third drink has made them drunk.

They take a table for four. Just as they're finishing dinner, the man who took you last night walks into the restaurant. He discreetly signals and sits by himself.

"Shall we go upstairs?"

One of the hotel waiters shows you to a room. Without being asked, you walk over to your customer to offer him your breasts. You're slightly astonished to see how easy it is to offer your tits to this unknown man.

He tells you to undress, then stops you. Your irons impress him. As he's pulling his cock out of your asshole he says, "If you're really good, I'll give you a fat tip."

There's no possibility that anyone'll love you anymore or that love matters. Because there's no hope of realizing what you want, you're a dead person and you're having sex.

He leaves before you're out of bed, leaves a handful of bills on a small white table. You walk back to the house after having neatly folded the bills and stuffed them in your cleavage.

Your chains are disappearing.

You can decide now whether to get dressed or not.

You can decide now whether to work for money or not.

You can decide now who to talk to.

He still whips you every day. When you complain another girl says, "You want to be whipped so why are you being querulous? You're not Justine."

Who you are is obvious. There's no one else but you. If you want to get whipped, like being whipped, girl.

You own me.

You control me.

I have nothing to do with you.

You're a murderer.

There's no such thing as a terrorist: there're only murderers.

I'm a masochist.

This is a real revolution.

Sometimes men bring straight women into the brothel. These straight women act like they're not looking down on the whores they see and yet, underneath this fake understanding or liberality, pure fascination lies. Fascination can involve no such intellectual judgment. These women tremble in front of the whores. Their eyes secretly follow around the corners of the doorways. Their eyes pin themselves on the long upper thighs, the cunt hair that might show, is it wet? How does she act when she's . . . with a MAN? Does she spread her legs very wide? What tricks does she use to make the man love her? Is she real? Is her underwear filthy? Does she drink piss in her mouth? Is she just an orgasming machine? Is she just a sink-into-flesh machine? What's it like to be without brains? Not to have any worries about how to get along in life how to keep up respect (among men) how to manage my career and children how to maintain my image and underneath the im-age . . . ? What's it like to live in that one (animal) place?

I'm not like HER? I'm a person. The beautiful woman adjusts her face. Her left hand lightly brushes over the top of her man's hand to show she and he are real: she's his woman because they're a twosome: real people in a real working world unlike these HOLES who DON'T EXIST.

You're watching the girls in the brothel:

A slender but well-proportioned girl, all white against the cunt-blood hangings, shaking, bearing on her hips for the first time the purple crop furrows. Her lover is a thin young man who's holding her, by her shoulders, back on the bed, the way Rene had held you, and watching with obvious pleasure and agony as you open your sweet burning belly to a man you've never seen beneath whose weight the girl's moaning.

They belong exclusively to members of the Club; they give themselves up to unknown men; as soon as they're ready, their lovers prostitute them in the outer world for no reason at all.

Other girls prostitute only for money, don't have pimps, and will never leave prison.

One girl is left in the brothel six months, then taken out forever.

Jeanne lived in the brothel a year, left, then returned.

Noelle stayed for two months, left for three months, returned totally broke.

Yvonne and Julienne who like you get whipped several times a day will not leave.

A man's making love to you.

He's giving you a ring, a collar, and two diamond bracelets instead of your irons.

He's saying he's going to take you to Africa and America.

"No! No!" you scream. You can't bear to have anyone love you. You can't bear another person's consciousness. You don't want anyone in your distorted desolated life.

"You're now free," the streaked-with-gray-haired terrorist says to you. "We can remove your irons, your collar, and bracelets, and even erase the brand. You have the diamonds, you can go home."

You don't cry; you don't show any sign of bit-- terness. Nor do you answer her.

"But if you prefer," she goes on, "you can stay here."

The jellyfish is the rapist. When O was 17 years old her father tried to rape her when she told him he couldn't rape her he weeps, "Your mother won't fuck me, those boys don't respect you enough, I'm the only man who's respecting you." This night O has a nightmare. A huge jellyfish glop who's shaped into an-at-least-six-story worm is chasing her down the main sand-filled cowboy street. All of her WANTS to get away, but her body isn't obeying her mind. Like she feels she's caught in quicksand so her body is her quicksand.

Nightmare: her body mirrors/becomes her father's desire. This is the nightmare.

Then O had a number of S&M relationships with guys who dug their fingernails into her flesh slapped her face then jellyfish wanted to become her whinedabouttheirproblems wanted to become her. Then O almost killed herself by developing an ovarian infection.

Men are rapists because rape rope is something O doesn't want. Why do people kill? A person kills, not from impotence but because he or she doesn't see what he or she is doing. O had to either deny her father's sex and have no father or fuck her father and have a father. This event led O to believe that a man would love her only if she did something she didn't want to do. How can I talk about ignorance, what ignorance unknowing is?

A young prince enjoying the company of an enchanting woman; he receives a cup of wine, elixir of life, out of her hands.

Probably Timurid period, 15th century.

The period corrresponding roughly to the 15th century takes its name from the great conqueror Timur or Tamerlane, whose armies overran the Near East between 1365 and his death in 1405, and whose descendants held court in Persia for the next hundred years. The classic style introduced by Ahmad Musa had reached its apex under the Jalayrid Sultan Ahmad, who ruled at Baghdad till its conquest by Timur. After that his artists seemed to have taken service with the Timurid princes, especially Iskandar Sultan under whose patronage the Timurid style may be said to have been formed:

2. THE BEGINNINGS OF ROMANCE

The First Days

Timelessness versus time.

I remember it was dusk. The lamps began to appear against a sky not yet dark enough to need them. I was shy of my mother because when she was on ups she was too gay and selfish and on downs she was bitchy. When she changed from ups to downs was the best time to approach her.

I adored my actress mother and would do anything for her. "Sarah, be a good girl and get me a glass of champagne." "Sarah, I'm out of money again. Your father's horrible. You don't need an allowance: give me ten dollars and I'll pay you back tomorrow." She never paid me back and I adored her.

"I never wanted you," my mother told me often. "It was the war." She hadn't known poverty or hardship: her family had been very wealthy. "I had terrible stomach pains and the only doctor I could get to was a quack. He told me I had to get pregnant." "I never heard of that. You got pregnant?" "The day before you were born I had appendicitis. You spent the first three weeks of your life in an incubator."

The rest I know is little. My father, a wealthier man than my mother, walked out on her when he found out she was pregnant with me. Since neither she nor grandmama Siddons ever said anything specific about him, I didn't know who he was. I always turned to my mother and I loved her very much.

Mother didn't want me to leave her. I think she could have loved me or shown that she loved me if she had had more time or fewer obsessions. "I don't care if my daughter respects me. I want her to love me." She craved my love as she craved her friends' and the public's love only so she could do what she wanted and evade the responsibility. All her friends did love her and I, I lived so totally in the world bounded by her being her seemings, I had no idea we were a socially important family. I didn't know there was a world outside her.

There is just moving and there are different ways of moving. Or: there is moving all over at the same time and there is moving linearly. If everything is moving-all-over-the-place-no-time, anything is everything. If this is so, how can I differentiate? How can there be stories? Consciousness just is: no time. But any emotion presupposes differentiation. Differentiation presumes time, at least BEFORE and NOW. A narrative is an emotional moving.

It's a common belief that something exists when it's part of a narrative.

Self-reflective consciousness is narrational.

Mother wanted me to be unlike I was. I got 'A's in school—it wasn't that I was a good girl, in fact even back then I was odd girl out: school was just the one place where I could do things right—but mother said getting 'A's made me stand out too much. Otherwise I was just a failure. I felt too strongly. My emotional limbs stuck out as if they were broken and unfixable. I kissed mother's friends too nicely when they were playing canasta. I was too interested in sex. I wasn't pretty in a conventional enough way. I didn't act like Penelope Wooding. When I washed a dish, I wasn't washing the dish. Since I didn't know if mother was god, I didn't know if I loved her. My friends told me I perceived in too black-and-white terms. "The world is more complex," they said. I said, "I get 'A's in school." Unlike.

"What was my father like, mommy?"

My mother looks up from a review of her newest hit. In those days she always got fabulous reviews.

"I mean my real father." When I had turned ten years old, my mother had carefully explained to me that the man I called my father had adopted me.

"He was very handsome."

"What exactly did he look like?" I had no right to ask, but I was desperate.

"His parents were wonderful. They were one of the richest families in Brooklyn."

Talking with my mother resembled trying to plot out a major war strategy. "What did his family do?"

"I was very wild when I was young. You remember Aunt Suzy. I'd sneak down the fire escape and Aunt Suzy and I'd go out with boys. I'd let them pet." My mother was high on Dex. "Your father was very handsome, dark, I fell in love with him. It was during the war so everyone was getting married." My mother refused to say anymore.

When I asked grandmama Siddons about my real father, she said he was dead. I replied I knew he wasn't dead. She said he was a murderer.

Why is anybody interested in anything? I'm interested when I'm discovering. To me, real moving is discovering. Real moving, then, is that which endures. How can that be?

Otherwise I lived in my imaginings. If anyone

had thought about me rather than about their own obsessions, they would have thought it was a lonely childhood, but it wasn't. I had all of New York City to myself. Since mother was an actress we had to live in New York or London, and I hugged New York to me like a present. Sometimes I'd leave the apartment and walk down First Avenue to the magic bookstore of brightly-colored leatherbound books. Book- and dress-stores were magic places I could either dream or walk to. Then I walked up Madison Avenue and fantasized buying things. I walked down to Greenwich Village where the most interesting bookstore held all the beatnik poets but I never saw them. I had to happen upon what I wanted. I was forbidden to act on my desire, even to admit my desire to myself. Poetry was the most frightening, therefore the most interesting appearance. Once or twice a monthly afternoon I'd avidly watch a play I had no way of comprehending.

When it was all happening around me and I had very few memories of what was happening, I didn't need to understand and, if I had understood, I probably would have been too scared to keep moving.

Mother was a real actress. I never knew who she was. I had no idea until after the end that she was spending all of her money and, then, that she was broke. She had always been very tight with me: taking away my allowances, never buying me anything. She madly frittered away money. Suddenly, surprisingly, she asked me if I wanted gifts and she bought me three copies of a gold watch she liked. At the same time she owed three months' rent, two of her bank accounts were closed, all of her charge cards had been revoked.

The 800 shares of AT&T grandmama had given her were missing. She was becoming gayer and less prudish. I would have done anything for her. She didn't talk to me or to anyone directly. She lifted up her favorite poodle, walked out of the apartment house, and didn't return.

Do I care? Do I care more than I reflect? Do I love madly? Get as deep as possible. The more focus, the more the narrative breaks, the more memories fade: the least meaning.

In spite of these circumstances which brought me to Ashington House, I'm thrilled when I see it. Trees always make my heart beat quickly. Bronze chrysanthemums. Dahlias around a pond in which two ducks quack, black and gray. And the whistle low. Two long streets, along leaves, lead away.

My aunts Martha and Mabel greet me. I've never met then before.

They're very wealthy and they're so polite, they're eccentric. They tell me I'm going to meet my real father. I don't want to see him, I do I do. I know he's handsome.

Aunt Martha tells me he's away at the moment.

We stop, walking in front of a picture of my father. At least it's a picture of him. "Your father," Aunt Mabel comments, "was too adventurous. Wild . . . headstrong . . . Your mother was his first wife and you were his first child."

"Who's his new wife?"

"He's had three. Last year he killed someone, shot him, who was trespassing on his yacht. The family got him off on psychological reasons. After his six-month stay in a rest home, he just disappeared."

"Aunt Mabel's scared, dear," Judy's commenting on Punch, "that you have some of your father's wildness."

Despite my politeness, they know who I am.

"I really don't know very much, Sarah. But I don't think you should have anything to do with him."

"Your father," Aunt Mabel interrupts her sister, "acts unpredictably. He can be extremely violent. We have no way of telling how he'll act when he sees you. The family has decided to help you as much as we can, but we can't help you with this."

I don't know what I'm going to believe.

He—for there can be no doubt of his sex, though the fashion of the time did something to disguise it—was in the act of slicing at the head of a Moor which swung from the rafters. It was the color of an old football.

I called Jackson up and he came over immediately. He was a drunken messy slob, maudlin as they come which all drunks are, but that's what let him be the kind of artist he was. He NEEDED to suffer to thrust himself out as far as he could go farther beyond the bounds of his physical body what his body could take he NEEDED to maul shove into knead his mental and physical being like he did those tubes of paint. I not only understood, I understood and adored. I would be the pillow he would kick the warm breast he could cry into open up to let all that infinite unstoppable mainly unbearable pain be alive I would not snap back I would be his allower of exhibited pain so he could keep going. That's why he loved me. He didn't need brains. He didn't need intelligence he was too driven.

"You're so beautiful, so warm: I don't know why you want me."

"I don't want you cause you're famous, Jackson. That's why all those other people're eating you up, making you think you're only an image HISTORY (in New York City a person's allowed to be alive or human if he/she is famous or close enough to a famous person to absorb some of the fame) so now you can no longer paint unless you close up all your senses and become a real moron. I want your cock because you're a great artist."

He seemed to be crying for his entire life. "I always thought about you, darling, even before I knew you. Exactly who you are was my picture of you: you are the woman I wanted the woman I thought I could never have. Now I know you. Why do you want me? I'm a mess. I said to myself: I'll do anything I can, with myself with EVERYTHING, to make my work, I did it, I did do it, I really fucked up my health and my mind. I don't regret this, but now I'm a mess. Please, don't be naive."

I knew this man, whatever would happen and death was the least, would stick by me.

And 'she was given the real names of things' means she really perceived, she saw the real. That's it. If everything is living, it's not a name but moving. And without this living there is nothing; this living is the only matter matters. The thing itself. This isn't an expression of a real thing: this is the thing itself. Of course the thing itself the thing itself it is never the same. This is how aestheticism can be so much fun. The living thing the real thing is not what people tell you it is: it's what it is. This is the thing itself because I'm finding out about it it is me. It is a matter of letting (perceiving) happen what will.

My mother was dead. We knew that. She might

have been murdered or she might have killed herself, perhaps accidentally. The police had abandoned the case and I didn't know how to find out on my own.

None of my father's family made any show of mourning for my mother. The funeral was a ghastly comedy. I was the only one sobbing my heart out while around me, hordes of women discussed Joan Crawford and her daughter and canasta games. Every now and then, I remember, Aunt Mabel told me to hand the chocolates around to her friends. I was wearing a fuzzy lavender sweater. One middle-aged woman shook the sweater back and forth and screamed that she wanted my mother's apartment.

After that, for a few months, I had nightmares, not nightmares but those deeper where I'd screaming wake up because there are so many thoughts, the thoughts are unknown.

I realize that all my life is is endings. Not endings, those are just events; but holes. For instance when my mother died, the 'I' I had always known dropped out. All my history went away. Pretty clothes and gayness amaze me.

The next thing I knew I received a letter from my father saying he was journeying to Seattle to see me, and then, it seems just a few days later, but that's my memory, I was standing in an old wood bar, then I was sitting down, a roly-poly man not at all the handsome soul-eyed man in that little painting I had wondered on was telling me he distinctly remembered my mother. But he didn't sound upset about her and she had been obsessed by him. "Are you my father?" I finally asked. "No. I'm your father's first cousin." He began to proposition me. "Oh, where's my father?"

"He's not here yet." Then this roly-poly man told me he came from an immensely wealthy family. His daughter picked bums off the street and slept with them. These stories made me realize that my mother's bohemian and my weirdnesses, which I had thought the same as the rich's amorality, were only stinky bourgeois playfulness.

Lutetia is the foulest because poorest section of Paris. After Charles the Simple visits Lutetia, he's so disgusted he tears a plan of Lutetia in two and orders the split to be made into a wide avenue.

Yvikel the widower has a daughter Blanchine whose health is slowly declining. They live in the center of Lutetia. Yvikel does everything he can for his daughter and resolves when she dies he'll kill himself.

After the avenue is built and sunlight, hitherto unknown, floods their rat-trap, Blanchine begins to recover. She recovers. To celebrate his gratitude, Yvikel recreates the plan of Lutetia in silk. Charles the Simple's hand reaches out and saves the section.

Dr. Sirhugues discovers a therapeutic blue plant light. An enormous lens concentrates this light on the diseased person held still by a cylindrical cage or 'focal jail.' But the rays are too powerful for the person to bear. Finally Dr. Sirhugues finds that only Yvikel's ancient silk is able to absorb and render harmless the dangerous portion of these rays.

I don't think I'm crazy. There's just no reality in my head and my emotions fly all over the place: sometimes I'm so down, all I think is I should kill myself. Almost at the same time I adore everything: I adore the sky. I adore the trees I see. I adore rhythms. I . . . I . . . I . . . I . . . I'm I'm mine mine my. I can't I can't. I hate being responsible oh.

I don't care what people think; when they think they're thinking about me, they're actually thinking about the ways they act. I certainly don't want them to give me their pictures of me I like the ways animals are socially. I would rather be petted than be part of this human social reality which is all pretense and lies.

I expected my father to be a strong totally sexually magnetic daredevil, macho as they come, but he was kind and gentle. He must have been very ill when I first met him because he had had five heart attacks. But his great physical pleasures were still drinking on the sly from Aunts Martha and Mabel and eating half-a-pint of coffee ice cream before going to bed. He relied for his life on the roly-poly cousin Clifford Still.

He must have wanted Clifford and me to marry. He believed in a reality that was stable which justice formed. A man who worked hard earned pleasure. A woman who took care of her husband kept his love. Approaching, death, for I quickly realized my father was extremely sick, frighteningly had to destroy those bourgeois illusions.

As his sickness grew, he began to depend on me. He didn't want me to walk away from his bed. I had known so much sickness.

"Your mother led me a hard life, Sarah."

"You weren't together very long, daddy."

"It was a passionate difficult existence. She wanted me to wear out. I don't think that's fair. I never understood her and I had very little tolerance for who she really was: I adored a figurehead. It was my death or getting rid of her, and she wanted the career.''

''You thought you loved her.''

''She depended on me more than she knew.''

''People who don't have any sense of reality, daddy, live crazy. Other people don't understand why they act the ways they do. They survive because everyone survives.''

As death approached my father said his life was useless. Because he now mistrusted.

I watched everything and I swore I'd never marry a man I didn't love and I'd never live for security.

Everyone hates me. My mother may have been murdered. Men want to rape me. My body's always sick. The world is paradise. Pain doesn't exist. Pain comes from askew human perceptions. A person's happy who doesn't give attention to her own desires but always thinks of others. Repressing causes pain. I have no one in this world. Every event is totally separate from every other event. If there are an infinite number of non-relating events, where's the relation that enables pain?

All of my family is dead. I have no way of knowing who means me harm and who doesn't.

The First Days of Romance

My father had left me all his possessions and I was, by the world's accounting, a well-to-do young woman. I owned a large house in Seattle. The rest of the money, since it was tied up in stocks and bonds and lawyers' incomprehensible papers, only meant that I was no longer untouchable. I knew most people wanted money or fame desperately just in order to survive. I knew I was no longer a person to a man, but an object, a full purse. I needed someone to love me so I could figure out reality.

The rest of my life was programmed for me: since I had inherited a house in Seattle, I would go to Seattle. Clifford, my father's best friend, was going to accompany me. I would never do what I wanted to do. My aunts Martha and Mabel would make sure that my money wouldn't allow me to act unreasonably and pleasurably. I was to grow accustomed to that reality.

My father died in the middle of January. It is now almost two years later. I can't describe Sutton Place—where Ashington House lay—for I miss it so deeply.

St. Agnes' Eve — Ah, bitter chill it was!
The owl for all his feathers, was a-cold;
The hare limped trembling through the frozen
*   grass,*
And silent was the flock in woolly fold;
Numb were the beadman's fingers, while he
*   told*
His rosary, and while his frosted breath,
Like pious incense from a censer old,

Seemed taking flight for heaven, with
out a death,
Past the sweet Virgin's picture, while his prayer
he saith.

It was snowing all the time. Frost covered the rooftops the trees the cars. People without hands walked slowly down the middle of the streets. Just as during the blackout, New York City had become a small happy town or a series of small towns strung out in a line. Whenever my mind looked in its mirror, it counted up its blessings: I was walking down a street. There was no one who was attacking me. There were no more stories or passion in my life. I had moments of happiness (non-self-reflectiveness) when I read books.

I knew there could be no way I would live with a man, because, while I desperately needed total affection, I wasn't willing to give up my desires which is what men want and I couldn't trust. The men who were part of my life weren't really part of my life: Clifford who I hated and the delivery boys who were weaklings.

Only sensations. What the imagination seizes as Beauty must be truth—whether it exists materially or not—for I have the same Idea of all our Passions as of Love they are all in their sublime, creative of essential Beauty . . . The imagination may be compared to Adam's dream—he awoke and found it truth. I am the more zealous in this affair, because I have never yet been able to perceive how anything can be known for truth by consecutive reasoning—and yet it must be. Can it be that even the greatest philosopher ever arrived at his goal without putting aside numerous objections? However it may be Oh, for a Life of Sensations rather than of Thoughts!

Of silks satins quilted satins taken from grandmother's bed thick satins black fur shorn from living lambs cotton steel wool the density of shit chewed-up cinnamon bark clustered angora and linen goose and duck feathers slumber

Of pyramid cheeses covered by red pepper overripe goat cheeses blue runs through the middle blue alternates with wine down the middle port sherry crumbled crumbling at fingertips' pressing no taste a physical touch sensation more than a taste the nose winding around itself

In front of the eye: red blue yellow green brown gray purple violet gray-blue violet-gray in various combinations or forms move by in a faintly maintained rhythm. These are the pleasures of the mind.

The mistake is allowing oneself to be desperate. The mistake is believing that indulgence in desire a decision to follow desire isn't possibly painful. Desire drives everything away: the sky, each building, the enjoyment of a cup of cappucino. Desire makes the whole body-mind turn on itself and hate itself.

Desire is Master and Lord.

The trick is to figure out how to get along with someone apart from desire if that's at all possible.

The body is sick and grows away from the perceiver. As old age comes the body gets sicker. All this is inevitable. When the body's sick, also the nerves are sick, the mind becomes sick because it no longer knows if it can trust itself. The scream no longer against pain, pain is now accepted as part of living, but against doubt begins.

I'm going to tell you something. The author of the work you are now reading is a scared little shit. She's frightened, forget what her life's like, scared out of her wits, she doesn't believe what she believes so she follows anyone. A dog. She doesn't know a goddamn thing she's too scared to know what love is she has no idea what money is she runs away from anyone so anything she's writing is just un-knowledge. Plus she doesn't have the guts to entertain an audience. She should put lots of porn in this book cunts dripping big as Empire State buildings in front of your nose and then cowboy violence: nothing makes any sense anyway. And she says I'm an ass cause I want to please. What'm I going to do? Teach?

Author: You're a dumb cocksucker. If some dumb person bought this book, he should have the grace to read it and if he doesn't like me, so what.

He (the author) has not hit the humors, he does not know 'em; he has not conversed with the Barthol'mew-birds, as they say; he has ne'er a sword-and-buckler man in his Fair, nor a little Davy to take toll o' the bawds there, as in my time, nor a Kindheart, if anybody's teeth should chance to ache in his play. None o' these fine sights! Nor has he the canvas-cut i' the night for a hobby-horse man to creep in to his she-neighbor and take his leap there! Nothing! No, an' some writer (that I personally know) had had but the penning o' this matter, he would ha' made you such a jig-a-jog i' in the booths, you should ha' thought an earthquake had been i' New York! But these master-poets, they ha' their own absurd courses; they will be informed of nothing! Would not a fine pump upon the stage ha' done well for a property now? And a punk set under her head, with her stern upward, and ha' been soused by my witty young masters o' the Cop Station? What think you o' this for a show, now? He will not hear o' this! I am an ass, I!

Author: Huh? What rare discourse are you fall'n upon, ha? Ha' you found any friends here, that you are so free? Away rogue, it's come to a fine degree in these spectacles when such a youth as you pretend to a judgment.

What is this that we sail through? What palpable obscure? What smoke and reek, as if the whole steaming world were revolving on its axis, as a spit?

Sailors, who long ago had lashed themselves to the taffrail for safety; but must have famished.

"Look here," said Jackson, hanging over the rail and coughing, "look there; that's a sailor's coffin. Ha! Ha! Buttons," turning round to me. "How do you like that, Buttons? Wouldn't you like to take a sail with them 'ere dead men? Wouldn't it be nice?" And then he tried to laugh, but only coughed again.

"Don't laugh at dem poor fellows," said Max, looking grave. "Do' you see dar bodies, dar souls are farder off dan de Cape of Dood Hope."

"Dood Hope, Dood Hope," shrieked Jackson, with a horrid grin, mimicking the Dutchman, "dare is not dood hope for dem, old boy; dey are drowned and d...d, as you and I will be, Red Max, one of dese dark nights.": THE ONLY CERTAINTY

To prove that there was nothing to be believed; nothing to be loved, and nothing worth living for; but everything to be hated, in the wide world.

Sir, my mother has had her nativity-water cast lately by the cunning men in Cow-Lane, and they ha' told her her fortune, and do ensure her she shall never have happy hour, unless she marry within this sen'night, and when it is, it must be a madman, they say.

Why didn't Melville suicide?
He didn't want to.

Which was, to lead him, in close secrecy,
Even to Madeline's chamber, and there hide
Him in a closet, of such privacy
That he might see her beauty unespied,
And win perhaps that night a peerless bride,
Never on such a night have lovers met,

The old woman leads him through many halls to the bedroom. He hides and hiding watches the girl he's in love with. Around the window a carved representational frame stained glass the middle a shield the middle blood. The girl who's never fucked takes her clothes off. She falls asleep on her bed. The young man covers her naked tits with candied apples fruits creamy jellies cinnamon syrup dishes silver, and lies down beside her.

She doesn't wake up. "Now, Sarah, this is purely medicinal." He handed the full cup to me. "It'll warm you. You must be warmed. What you should have is a hot bath and climb into a warm bed. I'm afraid Parrot Cottage can't offer such amenities. Never mind. This is the next best thing."

I did what he wanted me to and I hated myself for doing it. I was feeling good because the hot liquid relaxed my body and my tension; this growing ease made me a traitor to myself.

I had to keep the joy growing to blot out my consciousness of what was happening to me. Sensuous beauty is its own perfect excuse, for it brings itself into existence. Constant unendable sensuousness—not passion, which destroys— allows neither time nor memory. Later what happened helped me to understand my own nature; and even later, I could remember. I knew that this glory will and always happens and has something to do with dislike.

There is a dreamlike quality: my body wants as simply as any dream action. The body that wants a man whom I remember I heartily dislike, Clifford Still, can't be my body and I'm not upset. I know he knows every pore of my body better than I do. He's tricky. He gets me to be who he wants.

He says it's love. I mutter something about the girl I've heard he's going to marry. He laughs, and his laughter excites me.

"She's here with me," he said. "She's Miss Sarah Ashington. I decided she was the one as soon as I set eyes on her."

We married, but I still wanted madly to tell him I was afraid. I did not love the man I had married. He had overwhelmed me and aroused a certain passion in me. For a deadly moment I had found him irresistible. I don't love him, I cried inside my mind. I hate the inside of my mind. I want loving kindness, tenderness, not this mad wild emotion which he makes me become.

He drops to his knees and kisses my brow my eyelids my throat. He is kissing my naked heart. His tiny hands are shuddering my naked heart and now he is beside me (he is whispering to me he is whispering into me) This whisper is an outside cool breath This whisper is controlling me this whisper is my breath

In Paris policemen wearing blue triangular hats walk past buildings smaller than themselves and murderers look like each other and wear black. The ornamentation of Venice is precise a fairytale. The Roman streets lie sunlit, though there's no sun, where rooms, above, wander into room after room so that inside is outside though

74

it isn't. Sometimes I murdered a man or a group of men murdered me. I never saw the details of their faces.

"Sarah, my love," he murmured, "didn't you know? It was meant to be.

"I raped you," he said.

I stared at him incredulously.

"I want you to realize what a resourceful husband you have. You know how thick these winter fogs become? It occurred to me it'd be easy to lose our way . . . to wander around and around. You would feel tired. You wouldn't know what you were doing. I would make you drunk. I would be your savior. Under the guise of being God, I'd do what I want. You see how romanticism works."

"Is love always disgusting?" I was still regarding his perspective as useful.

He laughed. "What do you say, my pet? What does your body say when I touch it? I'm a man, Sarah; I'm not the mealy-mouth you think you want. You'll never know who I am."

"I still think it's disgusting you raped me and you planned to rape me."

"Your heart is telling you the truth," he said.

I didn't know if I loved my husband, or not.

I hated him I hated him but I knew if he should leave me I would die.

"My Madeline! sweet dreamer! lovely bride!
  "Say, may I be for aye thy vassal blest?
"Ah, silver shrine, here will I take my rest
  "After so many hours of toil and quest,
"A famish'd pilgrim, -sav'd by miracle.
  "Though I have found, I will not rob thy nest
"Saving of thy sweet self; if thou think'st well
  "To trust, fair Madeline, to no rude infidel.

Is my lover trying to murder me?

Is my lover trying to get my inheritance?

Is my lover a stupid worthless being?

"You have to trust me," he tells me. He won't tell me why. As soon as he tells me I have to trust him he takes some of my jewels, not my favorites, to sell because we can use the money, and when I ask him where the money is he won't answer me.

It's always my fault.

The nightmares have begun again.

As I said, it was winter. Three days after the winds started they could never stop for the concrete buildings housed them the streetlights held them the very beds and streets were winds. My skin and the stuff under my skin tremble, feel the temperature extremes, I don't know what is physical doubt and what is mental doubt.

I want vision. If I do everything I can to change myself (my SELF is my desires and dreams), so I don't have to leave this man—if I leave him, I won't bother again with a man—am I turning away from all that is dearest and deepest: vision? Or is vision that which has nothing to do with the will, but is necessity working itself out?

When I was in eighth grade, I thought the twins in my class, who were the only girls considered to be as intelligent as me, absolutely evil. I thought about them or absolute evil all the time. My husband wants me to put my inheritance in a joint bank account and draw up a will in his name.

How do we know how to act? How do we know when our actions will cause pain? How is it possible to chose? I knew I must not choose and I must escape.

Ye winds, ye cold air-snakes who wind through flesh, all who are nature:

Timelessness versus time.

There is very little money available to poor people. Since the American culture allows only the material to be real (actually, only money), those who want to do art unless they transfer their art into non-art i.e. the making of commodities, can't earn money and stay alive. Almost every living artist who keeps on doing art has family money or at least one helpful sex partner. There're a few artists whose work this society desires, for the country needs some international propaganda (and there's nothing as harmless to a materialist as formalist experimentation). So an American artist has about one chance in 100,000 to earn a living making art. Nevertheless all the artists expect to have this one in 100,000 success. After five to thirty years of either slow starvation or, if there's family or sexual money, lack of feedback recognition and distribution (for only the few artists who are famous get their work amply recognized and distributed), at least three-quarters of the artists who haven't died off yet are willing to do anything to succeed and turn to more commercial or technical work or become bums. Nevertheless, more and more people in urban America want to become artists because only artists are happy and know reality and there are no other jobs. The art market is becoming more glutted and artists help each other out less and stab each other in the back and do everything else necessary to survive.

There's a very good artist (i.e. he wants to do

art and nothing else) who wants the world to be as it is in the center of his art. All the artists recognize this goodness. He's very animal especially his wiggling ass he's such a great fuck, all the women artists want to fuck him. He lives in Seattle. He's fucked every woman artist in Seattle. All these women artists are still in love with him. A new woman artist who's more famous than these other women artists cause she's from New York City comes to Seattle. All the artists love her cause she's still living outside that community, isn't yet competing. She marries M. de Cleves so she can stay away from New York City.

As soon as these two artists meet, they fall madly in love with each other. The good artist isn't making art anymore because he can't work for money and do art, he refuses to starve to death, he refuses to do his art as anyone else wants him to do it, he refuses to butter up the ego of the one dealer in Seattle who shows new young work. The Princess is making lots of art because she's a quarter of a half successfully developed an image in New York. But she won't stop doing her art to support the purer artist even though this refusal makes her feel guilty. She doesn't love her new husband M. de Cleves.

Young people are now getting married cause they see how their parents followed every desire and got totally disrupted and how the total nihilism of 1979 caused nothing but O.D.'s and cancer. The Duc de Lorraine's going to marry Mme. Claude de France, the King's second daughter. Elizabeth of France wants to marry the Duc de Nemours.

The few male artists who're successful want to fuck girls twenty or more years younger than themselves. Why do men want to fuck and marry girls who're so dumb there's no interesting conversation or power play? Mme. de Cleves' mother says: studying human history answers you. If you want to understand an event, always increase its (your perceptive) complexity.

Historical example: Our former King met Mlle. de Pisselieu when she was extremely young and fell wildly in love with her. He fell in love with the Duchesse de Poitiers and kept hold of Mlle. de Pisselieu. His first son was poisoned. Because he bitched about his second son to the Duchesse de Poitiers, she said she'd make this son fall in love with her and did. The King's support of his third son, the Duc d'Orleans, made the second and third son hate each other. Mlle. de Pisselieu became the Duchesse d'Etampes. The King and the Duchesse d'Etampes hated the Duchesse de Poitiers. The Duc d'Orleans died from fever. The King died. Since the second son, our King, worshipped the Duchesse de Poitiers, he wanted to exile her lovers; but he adored her so much, he couldn't. Even as she got older, he would remain in love with her. He made her main lover Governor of Piedmont, but used the Vidame de Chartres to prevent this lover from getting anything. The Duchesse de Poitiers hated the Vidame de Chartres and the rest of his family. The Vidame de Chartres' niece just married the Prince de Cleves.

There is purity. The whole world, not in itself but as the beliefs that there are no qualitative differences between events so money takes the place of value, hates purity. Purity is always. There's no duality so purity is phenomena. But (relations): a story. A story plus a story plus a . . . makes . . . a tapestry. Human perception (relation) makes more perception. How can purity be a story?

Because all the male artists she knows fuck any cunt they can get into and the non-artist males bore her, the female artist doesn't believe love or purity's possible in this world and so sticks with her husband.

She learns from history that purity comes from lies or impurity: historical example: after Mme. de Tournon lived with a poet who made her support him by working dirty movies and in a sex show, she swore she hated men. She would always be a lesbian, even though she wasn't sure she physically liked fucking women as much as men, so she could devote herself to her art. Her former husband, Peter, was still in love with her even though she was a lesbian. Paul told Peter he was fucking ten different women because he was so horny. Peter was the only person in whom he dared confide. If his girlfriend found out, well: when his ex-wife had found out he had fucked just one other woman, she had an epileptic fit tried to commit suicide and broke up their marriage. The next morning, Mme. de Tournon repeated this gossip to all her girlfriends one of whom was Paul's girlfriend. Jean-Jacques told everyone Mme. de Tournon planned to marry him. Jeffrey knew Mme. de Tournon planned to marry him. Mme. de Tournon is known as the most honest female artist in Paris.

Mme. de Cleves realizes M. de Nemours has fallen in love with her even though she's married and he, being an artist, doesn't give a shit about other people's feelings.

The myth of art: artists have to do everything they can to do their art. They can't allow any desire to stop them from working. They have to deny themselves any lasting pleasure. If and when they fall in love, they destroy their lover or else transform their love into distaste or despair. So artists tend to love either objects or people who run away from them. So the female artist rejects the good male artist.

Historical example: Peter fell madly in love with Kathy even though she was married. Kathy told Peter since the law is worthless because all politicians are crooked Peter could marry her without her divorcing. Though Peter was morally middle-class, his desire made him embrace this defiance. He ran himself ragged for Kathy for six years while she fucked every artist in existence because she wanted someone richer especially more famous than Peter so she could become famous. Peter kept his jealousy secret. Kathy and his mother augmented this insecurity by repeating to him he wasn't rich or famous enough. When he started becoming rich and famous, which was what Kathy wanted, this jealousy springing out made him viciously turn to a young girl who was in love with someone else and kill Kathy. He was so rich and famous, he got away with it. He fell in love with a Mafiosa and whipped her. At the same time he loved many other women and, partly due to the cocaine his girlfriend was freely giving him, later killed several wives.

The end of hatred. Of that myth of art. The female artist can now love.

Cezanne allowed the question of there being simultaneous viewpoints, and thereby destroyed forever in art the possibility of a static representation or portrait. The Cubists went further. They found the means of making the forms of all objects similar. If everything was rendered in the same terms, it became possible to paint the interactions between them. These interactions became so much more interesting than that which was being portrayed that the concepts of portraiture and therefore of reality were undermined or transferred.

Three different power groups: the owners of the North-Eastern banks, the top-ranking military, and the Southern oil producers and distributors control the American government. The female artist doesn't know who her father is. Three months before she was born, her father had abandoned her mother and, according to her mother, had never tried to see her again or her daughter because he's a robot. She knows her father's name because a good friend of hers traced him. He is the secret head of the North-Eastern power coalition. Not even the American people know who he is.

As head of the North-Eastern power coalition he often uses the CIA for his own purposes. He once, through the CIA, hired the good male artist. He sent the male artist's wife on a suicide mission to Cuba. The female artist learns the good male artist's artistic status is a cover for being a hit man, that's why he's so pure.

Even though many of the New York City art patrons are also part of the North-Eastern power coalition, they're trying to do her father in because he supports Rockefeller and they want to throw their weight behind Reagan. They use the Marlborough Gallery as one of their fronts.

The female artist's husband from whom she's separated used to fuck her mother. Her father, discovering them, kills his wife in a jealous rage. The lover revenges himself by marrying the daughter, cutting her off from her father. Now the husband loves her because he's part of the

North-Eastern Reagan group and wants to use her to do her father in.

The female artist still thinks art is the only purity. The North-Eastern art patron group videotapes and even stage-manages every bedroom and intimate scene they can for info and blackmail purposes. The porn tapes they have no (more) use for they sell as high art. One very famous artist in New York City is very fond of privately commissioning and buying these snuff films. The female artist learns her father murdered her mother. While she's still confused, the art patrons get her even dopier then show her videotapes of the good male artist fucking every female in sight, for the good male artist sticks his cock into anything eight-and-a-half inches (the length of his cock) or less away from him. Since the female artist doesn't know who or what to believe anymore, art is nothing, she, throwing herself into her husband's arms, tells him everything. She doesn't know he's the main villain against her father.

Any action no matter how off-the-wall—this explains punk—breaks through deadness. When the good male artist overhears her telling her husband everything, even though he doesn't trust her, he suspects the politicians are trying to do them both in.

In New York City, when the 14th precinct is busting up 42nd Street, there's a special court called the obscenity court. The Mafia and this one Jewish guy who's their friend own the sex shows and shops which line 42nd Street. The shows and shops pay the D.A.'s office their monthly alimony. The D.A.'s office—no dumb cop can bust on his own—orders the local cops to break up a store only when the D.A.'s office needs some publicity, for instance to help the tourist trade, or when a high-high in the police office's retiring and some semi-high knows if it's schmeared all over the front page of the *Daily News* that he's cleaning up 42nd Street he'll get the job. The D.A.'s office warns the bosses there's going to be a bust and pulls only the shit workers in. Nevertheless a 42nd Street boss wouldn't be seen (much less CAUGHT) dead in one of his own shops or shows cause some cop might, being as stupid as he's reputed to be, not recognize this bigshot.

Ten peep-show machines fill the downstairs of a typical 42nd Street store. Occasionally a ghost businessman sticks shit-smeared razor blades into one of the slots. Upstairs a phony sex show for businessmen and men too old to get off any other way runs for a half hour once every hour and a half. These shows provide an important and unnoticed social service.

The obscenity court was filled to the till. The illegal alien India Indian who took the sex show tickets was swearing everyone in the store including the customers was responsible for the store's disgusting activities except for him. Two illegal Haitian aliens who ran the store's dirty film projectors for half minimum wage because they were aliens and didn't know better and if they complained they'd get deported and they couldn't speak English anyway and the male and female hippies who had been doing the sex show when the store got busted (they actually hadn't been doing anything but looking at each other and making dumb sounds cause the male hated touching women and the female had such a bad ovarian infection she'd be screeching with pain if either touched or if one bit of the pain-killing synthetic morphine she was shelling out $100 a week for to kill the pain so she could keep working to pay for the pain-killer wore off—if it all wore off): they were all silently awaiting their trial. When he hired them, the boss promised to pay to get them off if they were busted. It was a small room.

The judge entered so everyone in the room stood up and swore in loud voices. Everyone sat down. Two young women who both had lots of curly white hair were told to stand. The judge asked if anyone was representing them. A skinny, obviously hating Legal Aid with a folder in his hand stood up and said he was representing them (since there was no one else). The skinny representative needed ten minutes to find out who these ladies were. It was very hot in the courtroom. Then the skinny black-suit walked up to the judge. The judge and the skinny black-suit talked in whispers. The skinny Jew told the black women to step forward. While they stepped forward the judge recited some numbers at them and the skinny lawyer recited some numbers back. Then two guards pushed the women to the back of the room behind the judge's huge wooden stand. The room was very hot. The people weren't allowed to talk out of respect for the judge and the process of justice. The next accused were two black men. The first black man didn't seem to understand what was happening around him. His Legal Aid lawyer told him to plead guilty because he couldn't get off. He said "I'm guilty" though he wasn't sure what he was guilty of and the judge recited some numbers and his lawyer recited some numbers back. An armed guard pushed him to the back of the room. All of the defendants except for the India Indian Haitian and hippy sex show workers were black and all of the Legal Aid lawyers who didn't know their clients told their clients to cop pleas. The only other language used was mathematical so no one would get the wrong idea.

It must have been noon the sunlight was so bright even through the huge gray-filth-painted windowpanes when the judge called the hippy male and female to the bench. The hippy male was wearing a Bill Blass suit. The hippy female was wearing a middle-price gray suit with an ascot. They wanted to show the judge they were a cut above his usual defendant. The boss, the Jewish 42nd Street entrepreneur, had given them one of his own lawyers. The lawyer and the judge were whispering numbers. The hippies didn't hear a word. Then the boss appeared and walked up to the judge. Reaching into his pants pocket, he pulled out a huge wad of huge bills. He clearly flipped his wad in front of the judge's face and asked, "Haven't I paid you enough?" "Not here," the judge loudly replied. The lawyer and the judge said numbers again. The matron pushed the hippies to the back of the room where a small wood door led them to a hall. Out of the court of justice.

Before she worked the sex show she had earned all the money she needed especially the money for all the medicines by starring, she was either the only one or one of two, in sex films. She had thought of earning her money this way because when she had gone to a top Eastern university a doctor friend had told her her face was ravishingly beautiful. She had gotten these beginning model jobs by looking in the back pages of the *Village Voice*. Then men had told her she was too nice a girl to be an escort and why didn't she go back to school or they pulled her leotard away from her breasts and told her her breasts were too large or too small. She was very ashamed of her breasts. She hadn't been getting money for a while and more important than money, though that's all-important, she had to keep working to show herself she was surviving whatever she had to do. When you have to survive, thinking's either a luxury or a way, if you control it, to make what's necessary enjoyable. One day, answering an ad, she walked into a West Village basement apartment. The photographic set-up looked expensive. The black photographer told her he needed some nudie stills for the tops of playing cards. Since it was easy money, she said O.K. He showed her the cunt and cock on top of each playing card. She says she'd return with her boyfriend with whom she always worked twosomes. "No," said the photographer as he locked the door behind her, "we're going to use your cunt and my cock." "How can we do that?" she asked. "I'm very co-ordinated." She told him she had bad gonorrhea and he said he'd use a rubber. She figured if she had to get raped, she might as well remain healthy. "This won't take long," replied the photographer. While the big man was shoving himself into her, the girl lay as stiff as a log and wouldn't allow herself to feel any pleasure because this was the main way her fear would allow her to express anger.

NIGHT

I'm sitting in a window recess. The sinuous folds of a silk curtain hide most of my body. The lights of this silver and wood splendid loft-space sparkle as if they aren't giving off illumination but are burning only themselves up in the otherwise complete blackness. This anonymity is life. Here milling about turning around eyes go here and there while tongues move in the same direction all to look all to show disguise every dress must be the most beautiful every nipple must be the tautest the few flowers that exist are dead red isn't blood but rouge used as mascara: the quick movements of the cheekbones: the hair that making the skin as rigid as itself makes the face invisible: the fingernails painted by hundred-dollar-a-bottle polish create the only light the only whisper only the froth. This is the province of the ones who think they live their dreams. The richest, the most famous, the most audacious: now and then a person may allow desire. The sudden swerve of the eyes at the mention of a certain sale, the quickening of I, the casually filthy blue jeans worn over the knees of someone explaining he's making history, hard cocks a quick jet of blood, the cats stand high above complete the giddiness of this mass whom everything seductive the world can hold intoxicates; cold white and general inebriation play upon the already-fevered mind.

I want to be one of these vanguard people so I disguise myself:

Portrait In Red

Clifford does short-haul truck work. He doesn't work out of the hall; he has to call in every day to find out whether he goes to work or not. He must work ten hours in a row when needed and, then, if there's further work, can choose to do it. He often works a fifty-hour week. He says he's an artist. He says he doesn't have any time to make his art. He says his lines are his language. He is traditional and not avant-garde because he is just putting down what he sees, about which, because nobody else sees this, he can't talk to anyone.

At 7:00 A.M. the radio begins playing rock'n'roll loudly. Clifford pisses over the toilet, forgetting to lift the toilet seat, dials a phone number, says "Cliff", hangs up the phone. Whatever woman he's living with at the moment turns on the light over the bed, out of the bed makes herself a cup of tea and puts some oatmeal flakes and a cup of boiling water over the pilot so she can have oatmeal when she wakes up again at noon. They avoid talking to each other or else they'll quarrel. He says, "Have a good day," as he walks out the door. She does her best to get back to sleep.

He spends the early part of every evening in a bar, (even though he doesn't have time to read) he stares at a book he just bought as if it's a precious object. Other times he sits silently and smiles. He acts very friendly to the people he knows casually. Then he goes out to dinner, or he returns home and falls asleep. If he's in a bad mood, he stops perceiving the outside.

On the weekends he likes to go to fancy restaurants because they make him feel like he's a rich man and not encaged. He taught himself how to order good wines and wear designer suits. He won't go near cheap stuff. He doesn't want to live a groveling beggar's life. He discusses his political beliefs, describes various political events and his personal plans for the future.

I'm scared of Clifford.

I don't know anymore why I'm scared of him.

He hates me.

He does his best to hurt me he doesn't hurt me just out-front he does that too he sets me up: he acts nice (and when he's charming he can be REAL charming and I'm a sucker for that) and so I open to him I say, "Oh yes darling I do love you. I'll do anything you want." Because when I love a man especially when I'm being fucked well I'll do anything for him, otherwise I hate men I don't hate them, I just don't want them touching me cause their fingertips burn. Then we're sitting at a fancy restaurant in front of everyone in a loud voice he starts detailing exact examples showing what a shit I am

(The woman sits down at a small white-cloth-covered table.)

CLIFFORD: You're not able to love.

SARAH: I loved you.

CLIFFORD: You never loved me. You don't know how to give anything.

SARAH: I moved to Seattle and gave up my career, everything in New York, just to stay with you. I gave you all that money. Why did I do that?

(They're speaking so loudly all the middle-aged married couples in the restaurant are staring at them.)

CLIFFORD: I don't know. You had your own

reasons.

SARAH: What reasons are those? I don't know what they are.

CLIFFORD: I don't know. You know them. You tell me I have to grow up. YOU have to grow up.

SARAH (realizing she's going to cry): Excuse me. (She stands up. Starts to shake more and more.) I have to go to the bathroom. (Looks around the restaurant.) Where's the bathroom? (Wanders around the restaurant. Fake red velvet covers all the walls. Can't find a bathroom. Sits down again.)

CLIFFORD: Now, are we going to have a nice dinner? *I* want to have a nice dinner. (pauses) What books did you read today?

(The Chinese waiter approaches to take the order.)

CLIFFORD: I want the curried beef, the wonton soup, and the fried dumplings.

SARAH: Uh . . . Uh I, I . . . don't want anything. I'm not really very happy. Thank you.

CLIFFORD: You're going to eat. I'm not going to watch you get sick again.

SARAH: Yes, uh, eat. Eat. (To the waiter) I'm sorry. I'm really sorry. I'm sorry. I will eat. I have to eat something.

CLIFFORD: The sweet-and-sour shrimp.

SARAH: No, no, please waiter. I hate sugar. The shrimp in garlic sauce. (The waiter, obviously despising these louts, walks away.)

SARAH: I'm sorry. I just don't like sugar.

CLIFFORD: Get what you want. I'm getting what I want. If you like, you can eat a fried poodle.

SARAH: No.

CLIFFORD (expansively): Get five dishes six dishes. I'm paying. The thing is you can't take it. You hand it out you hand it out hard, but you can't take it. (Realizing what's coming, she can't hold her sobs back anymore.) I'm just telling you the way you really are.

SARAH: I never said anything to hurt you. All I ever said, again and again, and I say it right now, is that you have to get your life together. You have to quit trucking so you can do art full-time. Is that saying something against you? I've only got your welfare in mind.

CLIFFORD: You can't take anything rough as I can. You're weaker than me. You're not the woman I expected. You're not the woman I want. You're physically sick all the time.

SARAH: I AM weak. I never pretended I was different. I act publicly like I'm strong it's just an image and now I do it well I HAVE to survive. It isn't real. That's why I have to be alone so much. I have to be alone so I can be myself. It isn't that I don't love you. I just have to be alone.

CLIFFORD: I understand that you're weak. I want a strong feminist.

SARAH: Maybe you should go with someone else. (Hopefully)

CLIFFORD (resigned): Stop crying and eat your dinner. You need to eat. You're going to make yourself sick again.

SARAH: Please don't keep hurting me.

CLIFFORD: I'm trying to have a nice dinner. You keep bringing these matters up.

SARAH: I . . . ? I . . . (tentatively, obediently, takes a spoonful of food)

Since my crying is increasing this viciousness, I don't know how to stop it. I'm in terror.

He mirrors whatever I feel, but doesn't realize he's doing this.

:Johnny, I know you're going to murder me.

:I'm going to murder you, honey.

:I don't want you to murder me.

:But I want money and you've got it.

:You'd murder me even for just the little money you can get. (This isn't really a question.) I guess if you want to make love, we might as well make love. I'm horny.

:Can't you get to sleep? (His finger softly draws a line along her right-side chin bone.)

:I'm really tense.

:I'll kiss you and you'll go to sleep.

:I don't want to go to sleep. Where are you?

:I'm just playing.

:Come up here and fuck quickly and then go back to your play. (Johnny crawls up on the bed and very slowly, very gently, kisses her soft lips.)

:I just want to fuck. I don't want to kiss.

:I have to do something to relax you.

Portrait In Red

Red everywhere. Red up the river, where it flows among the green pines and old mining camps; red down the river, where it rolls defiled among the tiers of the shipping and the dock pollutions of a going-to-be-great (and going-to-be-dirtier) city. Red on the rain marshes, red on Queen Anne Hill. Red creeping into each of the abandoned cabooses; red creeping over the half-torn-away train tracks and lying on each weed; red climbed over the hacked-up docks into the commercial steel ships. Red in each long-shoreman's eyes when he returns home and slaps his wife around red at the end of the cigarette butt red in the dynamite red of the fire. Red of the eyelid and nose flesh of the bums walking down

First Avenue past the more monetarily successful artists. Red the colors of the condos they're building over the bodies of old people who now have nowhere to live. Red the artist's hand not from paint but from striking his lover's face out of repressed fear.

The raw afternoon is rawest, and the red is most red, and the streets are filthiest on the part of Bell Street next to the river where I lived in fear of my lover for six months.

He didn't want to hurt me. There are many desires. But that desire was a fairly surface desire. He was very scared. The fear was very deep. The fear was he used to be on the skids he had to live when he was an adolescent by selling junk he had no one to turn to and he was a bum he was among bums no woman would want him. He wanted education. He got better and better women. He took each one for as much as he could before she had the strength or desperation to flee. He didn't want to be in this position again. He was desperate. He was a man. He was tough. He was honest. He didn't use people. He could take care of himself and he never needed anybody. All under this surface was fear. The tension between the two was unendurable especially for him.

Worse than this was the positive tool or wall he had built to keep surviving. He was as stubborn as a steel wall. As soon as he wanted he could be impenetrable. Impenetrable is stupid. Nobody could touch him. This steel wall was the most dangerous thing about him was total madness.

Women found him sexually attractive and then fled from him. He had had a series of women and could obviously get any woman he wanted who didn't know his reputation. Living with him was living with hell. He never relaxed. He was always like an atom bomb. He thought he was delicate feminine because when he got drunk (relaxed) the only aspect he could perceive was overwhelming self-insecurity or fear. And fear is feminine: for women it lies in the heart of heterosexual sex. I don't know whether I believe that.

I don't want to believe that.

CLIFFORD: Since the world is a hostile place to me, I have to be able to do whatever I want. I'm going to have a good time today. I don't care what you feel. You're probably dying because you're always dying as a ploy to get at me. To destroy me. I'm going to have a good time today. When I have a good time, I eat crepes and drink lots of cappucino, then I go to the department stores to look at either Ralph Laurens or Gucci suits. After six I drink champagne, beer with my buddies and shoot pool, I get good and drunk. I know I shouldn't get drunk like this everything is my fault it isn't my fault. A language that I speak and can't dominate, a language that strives fails and falls silent can't be manipulated, language is always beyond me, me me me. Language is silence. Once there was no truth; now I can't speak.

I'm going to Paris because in Paris no one speaks English. That's where I'll be able to make art.

I won't have any chance of making money there. I've never had steady money because I'm nothing. I hate this government because they're responsible.

I don't like women because I hate their cunts. I don't know who they are. I know I know who they are: they just want. They think they're perfect. I don't want to become better. I don't

96

care. I don't have problems as other people do.

I decided I wasn't going to have anything else to do with a woman. I wasn't going to try to live with one again. I was into my work and I didn't have the time.

I set up this living situation so no woman could enter it. I built that loft bed and no other conveniences anywhere, just my working tools. For a shower I go to the sauna down the street for ten dollars an hour. I eat my meals in the Belltown.

I know I drink too much. I like sex a lot. Once or twice a week this crazy girl when she can't pick any other man up that night comes around one or two in the morning. She doesn't want anything but sex from me and that's all I want from her.

I'm a teamster and I make a lot of money so I'm in a position to help out my fellow artists who aren't as financially well-established as I am. I buy their work whenever I can. I like to pay for their drinks. I'm generous.

SHE: What is his relation to money?
SHE: It stinks.

I kept thinking he was conning me. Then I would think, this is crazy and paranoid. I just want to know.

SHE: I want to ask you about Clifford. If you don't want to answer any of these questions cause they're too close, I fully understand. They're just so many times I haven't known the truth in a situation and this time I want to know the truth.

CLIFFORD: Let me explain something. Let me explain something. I absolutely want to explain something. I am not a violent person. I have never in my life physically hurt anyone. I would not hurt a woman. Nobody understands how sensitive I am. I do not believe all that shit about

97

men and women I think sexism is disgusting. Men who want women to do the housework and bow to them are pigs. I cry and I'm as sensitive as a woman. No one realizes this about me I don't have anything to do with the world. NO.

As a result of his own barrenness, he develops a capacity to absorb the fertility of others. Of the real self. The only way you can get the real self is to rip someone off. The only way you can get love. Humans need love. You're a con man.

When my girlfriend got sick, she was good and sick she was almost dying, I didn't give a damn because when she's sick she can't give me anything. She had become sick so she could deny me. This means the sicker she becomes, the more I have to rip her off. That's the only way things are fair between us. I'm a feminist. I don't want a woman mothering me or telling me what to do. I want a balance of power that's why I have to take from her.

I didn't bother to lie and she knew I was taking from her. But she played stupid, asked me if I was ripping her off why was I ripping her off. She not only played stupid she played the martyr. She kept whining while I was sleeping and I need my sleep I work like a dog-shit every day trucking I don't have time for whining which is pretense She cried she was helpless since she didn't know anyone in this strange town, she was dependent on me, she was too sick to shop and desperate for food I was refusing to give her. I didn't want any part of this. I didn't starve her to death and I didn't throw her out. She was just asking me to let her be the boss so I wouldn't get anything from her and I wouldn't allow that. I appear stupid because I don't bother talking to people Their talking—like her sickness—is pretense

And I have to work my butt off. If I'm one thing, I'm absolutely honest.

From being sick, she goes on to act like she's scared of me. I guess she is or she really thinks she is. I'm too worn-out to know the difference. I don't give a damn about taking care of her anymore because she's made me give up. Because she's done me in.

I'll tell her something. She doesn't know how to love somebody. Psychiatrist said about. Say I'm violent.

I think I understand but nobody agrees with me.

I'm not going to let her get away from here because otherwise so I've locked this door. I know I shouldn't lock this door but she's not really locked in.

Two beautiful girls live in Paris. The oldest is tall and thin. Since her eyelids are always three-quarter's over her eyes, she appear to be constantly looking at the ground. This lack of curiosity or humility makes her seem nunlike. Pale skin with absolutely no color over the cheekbones emphasizes the sobriety.

The younger sister, unbelievably beautiful, radiant as a moon that has no night to contrast it, pink-orange roses in the cheeks and eyes, shining because they haven't yet been touched: not being caught in the maw of fame, not fearing the traps sexual satiety causes, not desiring beyond desire to be an image: real. Her hair would fly around her head like the feathers on some of those hats in the Blvd. St-Germaine Des Pres shop windows. Her emotions are even more uncontrolled, for no one has ever shown her she has to control herself or else she is hurt. These uncontrolled movements add charm. But she's so scared of her mother, she keeps this wildness to herself.

PORTRAIT IN RED, kept handing over this money

PORTRAIT IN RED if I ever asked about it he said

PORTRAIT IN RED $60,000 in debt and that's why

PORTRAIT IN RED how

PORTRAIT IN RED did your first husband rip you off for a quarter of a million dollars excuse me

PORTRAIT IN RED the last year Clifford and I were together, we both went to see a psychiatrist.

     : I didn't know that.

     : He said he couldn't do anything more for us as things stood: Clifford should definitely go into therapy.

     : Is he still doing a lot of drugs?

SHE: He's getting stranger and stranger these days. He just sits by the TV and doesn't move and never talks to anyone. We haven't talked in months.

SHE: Is he still doing a lot of drugs?

SHE: Drugs? You know I've lived with him for six months, but I don't really know anything about him. He comes home from work on the weekdays so dead tired. He can't talk. He immediately goes to sleep, wakes up, goes back to work. On the weekends he wakes up immediately, goes out of the house. He's gone for hours. If I ask him where he's been, I don't want to pry or anything I'm just trying to find some conversation, he gets so angry I don't ask.

PORTRAIT IN RED me was to take a razor blade and cut through this wrist in front of him.

     : How could you stand living with him for six years?

100

: It was only three years.

: Three years? He said six.

: From 1975 to 1978. My first husband and I were married for almost six years.

PORTRAIT IN RED draw blood and freaked out.

PORTRAIT IN RED used to.

PORTRAIT IN RED he kept telling me I was psychotic because I thought he was ripping me off and when there's only one other person there's no way to know.

3. THE END

I'm thinking about you right now and I've been thinking about you for days when I jerk off I see your face and I'm not going to stop writing this cause then I'll be away from this directness this happiness this isness which is. At the same time I'm never going to have anything to do with you again. Because you, even if it is just cause of circumstances, won't love me. This isn't the situation. I'm being a baby as usual. There are complications. Are shades, hues, never either-or, the shades are meanings, come out, you rotten cocksucker

44 B.C. Brutus and Cassius murder Julius Caesar.

42 B.C. The outlaws Brutus and Cassius in the Battle of Philippi lose to Mark Antony.

Mark Antony allies himself with Cleopatra and neglects his wife Octavia (Caesar's great-nephew's sister).

Messala, the main literary patron, goes with young Caesar who turns away from Antony.

31 B.C. The Battle of Actium young Caesar decisively defeats Antony.

29 B.C. Empire begins. Centralization of power which is thought. Any non-political action such as poetry goes against centralization. Ovid is exiled. Propertius and Horace are told they have to write praises of the empire.

To The Door

"**W**hy aren't you grabbing my cunt every chance you get? I love fucking in public streets and why are you telling me you want to be friends and work with me more than you care about sex with me, but you don't want FOR ANY REASONS to cut out the sex? So you want to own me without owning me?" says Cynthia the whore. She goes out on to the street to search for Propertius her boyfriend. It's night. She finds him.

"Why don't you take me? I don't have more than five minutes. Why does it have to last beyond these grabbing actions? Oh I believe in love that thing that is impossible to happen"

A bones-sticking-out cow is dragging a cart by glittering religious objects past a dead murderer

"And besides you're fat and ugly and I'm more beautiful than you and I've got more money (I can earn more in five minutes in this world): you should be taking me out to dinner.
Here's the hole the window we can climb through to the place we can fuck in. Holes."

He, rubbing his crotch: I just want to stick my dick into something. What the hell do I care, by all that stinks, what I stick it into? When I was a kid I used to use a bottle with something in it. Now I can use a cunt but unfortunately a cunt has a woman attached to it. By all that's holy, girl, I'm a man! The best wet dream I had was in high school I was fucking this girl I wanted to fuck, her hole disappeared, but I still kept shoving, rubbing into her. I woke up and I was pounding into the bed.

Actually I don't want you to have anything to do with me. I just want split-open red-and-black pussy.

CYNTHIA: Why don't you let me go: I want to go back to not-existing which is freedom.

HE: I like you a lot.

CYNTHIA: I'm lifting up my leg and peeing all over you. That doesn't work. Maybe if I let you make all the decisions, you'll be my father.

HE: I don't want to make any decisions. People tell me what to do real easily and I won't stand being told what to do so I avoid people.

CYNTHIA (to herself): But I want him to love me. He's never going to give me what I want, but I'll still fuck him.

They're standing in front of a huge partly open window through which is an empty space.

CYNTHIA: C'mon. Jump. What's the matter with you, dummy, are you too fat to jump? I've got five minutes. You're gonna be a creep and not do anything, I'm scared too, I want it. Flesh is it. Your arms are it.

HE: Isn't that guy waiting for you?

CYNTHIA: That's why we've got only five minutes.

AT A DOOR'S EDGE

During the night, the streets very dirty uneven rocks no way to be sure of your footing much less direction as for safety all sorts of criminals or rather people who had to survive hiding under one level of stone or behind an arcade you can't even see just standing there: there's no way to tell the difference between alive and dead. Criminalities, which are understandable, mix with religious practices, for people have to do anything to satisfy that which can no longer be satisfied

We shall define sexuality as that which can't be satisfied and therefore as that which transforms the person.

(Stylistically: simultaneous contrasts, extravagancies, incoherences, half-formed misshapen thoughts, lousy spelling, what signifies what? What is the secret of this chaos?

(Since there's no possibility, there's play. Elegance and completely filthy sex fit together. Expectations that aren't satiated.)

Questioning is our mode.

CYNTHIA: Just why are you fucking me? You've got a girlfriend named Trick and you love her. According to you she's satisfied with you and you with her.

Propertius is staring blankly at the door.

CYNTHIA: I'm sick of being nice to you. So what if you want a girl who'll consider you her top

priority and yet'll never ask you for anything? I
can't be her.

Propertius is staring blankly at the door and
scratching his head.

CYNTHIA: DON'T FUCK ME CAUSE YOU LIKE
THE SMELL OF MY CUNT. LEAVE ME ALONE.
This is the only way I can directly speak to you
cause you're autistic.

PROPERTIUS: This is my poem to your cunt
door.

> *Oh little door*
> *I love you so very very much.*

CYNTHIA: Well, everyone wants to fuck me I tell
you I'm sick of this life. Who cares if you're
another person waiting at my door? You're just
another man and you don't mean shit to me.

PROPERTIUS: Oh please, cunt, I'm cold and I'll
be the best man for you and I know you're fucking someone else that's why you won't let me near
you you cheap rags stinking fish who wants
anything to do with corpses anyway? (to himself)
And thus I tried to drown my mourning.

CYNTHIA: This is the kind of funeral I want goddamn you
    Now I'm dead. I want:
    One. Well my mother father and grandmother
are dead. Fuck that.
    Two. When my mother popped off, after-
wards, she lay in this highly polished wood coffin

the most expensive funeral house in New York City—where all the society die after they're dead—FAKE, everything was real but there are times real is fake, flowers, tons of smells, wood halls polished like fingernails; preacher or rabbi asks me "Do you know anything good I can say (I have to say something: SAY SOMETHING!) over your mother's mutilating body?" (it being understood that all society people are such pigs that . . .) and I tell him how beautiful she is; no one cries they're there to stare at me as I make my blind way through the narrow aisle, to number how hysterical I am did I really love her? The beginning of the funeral the family lawyer, having walked over to me, shakes my lapels, "Where are the 800 IBM shares?" "What 800 IBM shares?" "There are 800 missing IBM shares and no one knows how your mother died. I thought she gave them to you." "She never gave me a penny."

Three. I do everything for sexual love. What a life it's like I no longer exist cause no one loves me. So WHEN I DIE, I'll die because you'll know THAT YOU CAUSED ME TO DIE and you'll be responsible. That's what my death'll do to you and you'll learn to love. I'm teaching you by killing myself.

Four. You're gonna have to die too. You'll be like me. You'll be where I now am. Your cockbone will be in my cunt-bone.

Five. This is why life shits: Because you're gonna love me the second I leave you flat. Our sexuality comes from repression. When you reject me, I'm gonna die in front of you. In the long run nothing's important. This is the one sentiment that makes me happy.

Please be nice to me.

BARBARELLA: You've got to get a man who has money.

DANIELLE: I want money and power.

CYNTHIA and BARBARELLA (agreeing): Money and sex are definitely the main criteria.

DANIELLE: Sex?

CYNTHIA: I think I want a wife who has a cock. You understand what I mean. I don't understand why men even try to deal with me like I can be a wife, and then bitch at me and hurt me as much as possible cause I'm not a wife. Who'd ever think I'm a wife? Do you think I'm a wife? (Barbarella giggles.) But when I'm sexually open I totally change and this real fem part comes out.

BARBARELLA: I want a husband. No. I take that back. I want someone who'll support me.

CYNTHIA: Good luck.

BARBARELLA: I'm both the wife and husband. Even though none of us are getting anything right now, except for Danielle who's getting everything, our desires are totally volatile.

DANIELLE: I can't be a wife. I can be a hostess. If I've got lots of money.

BARBARELLA: One-night stands don't amuse me anymore.

CYNTHIA: I think if you really worship sex, you don't fuck around. Danielle fucks around more than any of us, and she's the one who doesn't really care about sex.

BARBARELLA: Most men don't like sex. They like being powerful and when you have good sex you lose all power.

CYNTHIA: I need sex to stay alive.

A street in Rome. The sky's color is deep dark blue. One star can be seen. Very little can be seen on the street—just different shades of black.

Now we're fucking:
I don't have any finesse I'm all over you like a raging blonde leopard and I want to go more raging I want to go snarling and poisoning and teasing eek eek, curl around your hind leg pee, that twig over there, I want the specific piss shuddering of the specific cock. I want, help me. I need your help.

Take off your clothes. Clothes bind. Clothes bind our legs and mouths and teeth, still shudder want too much, taking off our clothes

Why can't you ever once do something that's not allowable? I mean goddammit.

Hit me.

Do anything.

Do something.

Sow this hideousness opposition blood to everyone proud I want to knock Ken over with a green glass I want to hire a punk to beat up Pam I will poison your milk if you don't leave your girlfriend.

Sex is public: the streets made themselves for us to walk naked down them take out your cock and piss over me.

The threshold is here. Commit yourself to not-knowing. Legs lie against legs. Hairs mixing hairs and here, a fingerpad, a lot of space, a hand, a lot of space, hairs mixed with hairs, a real sensation.

Go over this threshold with me.

Thumb, your two fingers pinch my nipples while your master bears down on me. Red eyes, stare down on top of my eyes. Cock, my eyes are staring at you, pull out of the brown hairs. Red eyes, now you're watching your cock pull out of the strange brown hairs. Thumb, your two fingers pinch my nipples while your master bears down on me.

Now you've gone away:

Joel Fisher whom I thought hated me saw me every other day and Rudy whom I thought the worst that is the meanest of my boyfriends always called me every other day or at least let me call him. Peter who lives with another girl three thousand miles away from me and he adores her phones me at least once a month.

This guy doesn't care about me.

But when he looks at me, I know there's a hole in him he loves me. No, he doesn't. I can't do anything until I know whether he loves me or not. I have to find out whether he loves me or not.

You might as well accept you're in love with him because if you give him up just cause he doesn't adore you enough, you'll have nothing. In the other case, there's a 50% (or 30% or 4% or 1%) chance you'll keep touching his flesh.

Cynthia, sitting at her dressing-table in her little apartment overlooking the middle-class Roman whores' section, is dressing her hair:

That goddamn son-of-a-bitch I hope he goes to hell I hope he gets POISONED wild city DOGS should drive their thousands of TEETH-FANGS through his flesh a twelve-year-old syphilitic teenager named Janey Smith should wrap her cunt around that prick I hate that prick I hate those fingers I hate black hair I want his teeth to rip themselves out in total agony I want his lips to dry up in Grand Canyon gulfs I want him

114

paralyzed never to be able to move again and to be conscious of it:

Then, louse, you'll learn. You'll learn what it is not to know. I want you to learn what it is to be uncertain like I am. I want you to learn what it is to want like fire. The driest and coldest dry ice: the top of your head will burn and the rest of your body will freeze shake muscles will cramp like they do when they're not yet used to the bedless floor, at night, you will know agony.

You must learn what it is to want.

Thus says the whore who's unable to hold in and repress her emotions.

Among these women, free yet timorous, addicted to late hours, darkened rooms, gambling, and indolence, sparing of words, all they needed was an allusion.

I reveled in the admirable quickness of their half-spoken language which resembled more the suppressed diffused violence a teenager feels. These exchanges of threats and promises—as if once the slow-thinking male is banished every message from woman to woman is clear and overwhelming—are few in kind and infallible.

The first time I dined at her place, three brown tapers dripped waxen tears in tall candlesticks and didn't dispel the gloom. A low table, from the Orient, offered a pell-mell assortment of *les hors-d'oeuvre*—strips of raw fish rolled upon glass wands, *foie gras*, shrimp, salad seasoned with pepper and cranberry—and there was a well-chosen Piper Heidsieck brut, and very strong Russian Greek and Chinese alcohols. I didn't believe I'd become friends with this woman who tossed off her drink with the obliviousness a person caught in the depths of opium watches his hand burn.

This "master" was never referred to by the name of woman. We seemed to be waiting for some catastrophe to project herself into our midst, but she merely kept sending invisible messengers laded with jades, enamels, lacquers, furs . . . From one marvel to another . . . Who was the dark origin of all this nonsense?

"Tell me, Renée. Are you happy?"

Renée blushed, smiled, then abruptly stiffened.

"Why, of course, my dear Colette. Why would you want me to be unhappy?"

"I didn't say I wanted it," I retorted.

"I'm happy," Renée explained to me, "but the sexual ecstasy is so great, I'm going to be physically sick."

Propertius decides he doesn't want to fuck Cynthia again:

How can such a stinking fish a cunt who has experienced what it is to be the wish-fulfillment of many men hordes of men more men than serve the Great Caesar be innocent? My fantasy is special. Moreover she's had such a poverty-regulated life she can't have any life in her to be elegant with me: to give me the beauty that is female that I deserve. She isn't female, that elongation of steel triangles and bolts.

My girlfriend on the other hand, if anyone ever hurts me, is going to have to murder that person. For me. When I'm dying from a worn-out liver punctured guts three punches in the face and dirty track marks, I lived to the physical and mental hilts, my girlfriend will naturally die. On the other hand a whore goes from man to man; she's no man's girl. So there's no possibility I'm going to love you and if I fuck you, it's just cause

you're a present open cunt. The women's libera-
tionists are right when they want to get rid of all
hookers by imprisoning all of you whores.

CYNTHIA: I've been waiting for you.
PROPERTIUS: What the he . . . ? (Grabbing the
other girl into him.) Oh, hello. I'm busy now.
CYNTHIA: I just wanted to see you.
PROPERTIUS: I'm busy with someone now. I'll
give you a call tomorrow.
CYNTHIA: Please. (There's nothing she can do.)
OK. (Propertius and the dark-haired girl walk in-
to the house. One of the dogs on the steet starts
barking.)

The Street of Dogs. Two lines of houses lead to
a Renaissance perspective. These lines are
seemingly-only-surface connected three-story
townhouses. A sun and a three-quarter moon
hang over one townhouse. Common household
objects such as lamps, a part of a table, half of a
torn plastic rose kitchen curtain take up some of
the window space. Outside a townhouse a dog
leans over her basket of laundry. Two dogs, one
leaning farther out of his window than the other,
open their mouths to howl. Their teeth are sharp
and white and they have long red tongues. One
dog over her basket of wash gossips with another
dog. Two young dogs are mangling each other
next to the curb. On each side of the street the tall
thin windows form a long row.

Cynthia barks like a dog:
I can't help myself anymore I really can't I'm
just a girl I didn't ask god to be born a girl. When
I think, I know totally realistically I'm an alien
existant. I hate or have nothing to do with

everyone. I'm a whore. But I'm not thinking. You're just so cute. I have to get you out of my body. It'd be good for me to get you out of my body cause then I'd be strong that is single. I don't want to and why should I? I want to have this sweet thing that is you. I'm going to go after you, aching sore, (I don't care what your reaction is to me) because why not, darling?

She walks up to the door where Propertius lives and sits herself in front of it. Even though she doesn't care anything about him. He's never bought her a present.

The door doesn't move.

A big baldheaded half-naked man opens the door lays his palms on the doorway. Cynthia goes away.

You alone born from my most beautiful
carecure for grief
Shuts out since your fate
"COME OFTEN HERE"
Fiction by my will will become the most
popular form
Propertius, your forgiveness, peace,
Peter, yours.
to redefine the realms of sex so sex
I'm crawling up your wall for you.
I must face facts I'm not a female.
I must face facts I can't be loved
I must face facts I need love to live.
Hello, walls.
How're you doing today?
Hello, my watch.
Please watch over Propertius, you are here

118

because I will never get near him again.
He is now forbidden territory.

Cynthia lays down on the street and sticks razor blades vertically up her arm. The bums ask her if she needs a drink. Madness makes an alcoholic sober, keeps the most raging beast in an invisibly locked invisible cage, turns seething masses of smoke air into calm white, takes a junky off junk as if he's having a pleasant dream, halts that need FAME that's impossible.

I am only an obsession. Don't talk to me otherwise. Don't know me. Do you think I exist?

Watch out. Madness is a reality, not a perversion.

Propertius On The Nature Of Art

PROPERTIUS: If you read from end to end of the Greek Anthology, you won't find a love poem where the character of individuality of the woman who's loved matters.

(Goddamn sluts: if only the cunts were unattached; I like them but they're all crazy. They've got emotions. I like the one I slept with last night. She moans hard when I stick my cock in her. Does she have any idea what I think? I know I'm a macho pig why the hell shouldn't I be why should I be something I'm not I care about Writing. Their emotions and hysterics are all second-class existents.)

My woman is the black hole of vulnerability and takes everything from me and Not Human. She can take me wherever she wants me. I have to care for someone.

Women, I'll use everything I can get: I'll trample on your passions needs even if they cause you to die, I'll be as elephant-like as I can, and so the ugly is left as ugly and consciousness' unavoidable anguish is as it is in me. I am wide enough to let be.

My writing will cure you of your suffering. Give me five bucks, I come even cheaper I'm cheap, I'll tell you how to win the love of a person who doesn't love you. I'll tell you how to endure your rending when the girl you love spits in your face and fucks another man right in front of you.

AUGUSTUS (through the lips of his literary counselor Maecenas): You're not a poet, slime, because all your poems are about is emotion. A man who pays attention to emotions isn't a real man. We have the world to take care of: we have to make sure people have more than necessary access to food; we have to watch the greedy hawks who get into power and rape.

We are the teachers. If we teach these champagne emotions are worth noticing, we're destroying the social bonds people need to live.

PROPERTIUS: If my writing is going against social bonds, that's who I am. Shove your Empire and shove society.

MAECENAS: You're only dealing with your little obsession.

PROPERTIUS: You too, Maecenas, one day, are going to have to realize you're not rational and then in your desperation, ignorant, you'll turn to my words

Propertius runs away because he doesn't like making his privacy public. Public is an image a rigidity, and only as such is fun. He points to a mass of art-world figures, from his shadows, as they're entering a salon resplendent with gilding and illuminations, on in which they're instantly being welcomed by the most beautiful Roman bodies.

One of them has just revealed original talent and with this first portrait of his shows himself the equal of his teacher. A sculptor's chatting with one of those clever satirists who refuse to recognize merit and think they're smarter than anyone else. The people talk either about how they earn money or who's becoming more famous. All are grasping for good reason in these desperate times. Since the only ideas are for sale, none are mentioned. A few women appear to maintain the surface that sex is still possible. Eyes never see the mouths the faces are talking to.

Well you can say I write stories about sex and violence, with sex and violence, and therefore my writing isn't worth considering because it uses content much less lots of content and all the middle-ranged people who are moralists say I'm a disgusting violent sadist, Well I tell you this:

"Prickly race, who know nothing except how to eat out your own hearts with envy, you can't eat cunt, writing isn't a viable phenomenon anymore. Everything has been said. These lines aren't my writing: Philetas' DEMETER far outweighs his long old woman, and of the two it's his little pieces of shit I applaud. May the crane-who-delights-in-the-Pygmies'-blood's flight from Egypt to Thrace be so long, like me in your arms, endless endless grayness, may the death shots the Massagetae're directing against a Mede be so far: what is here: desire violence will never stop. Go die off, oh destructive race of the Evil Eye, or learn to judge poetic skill by art: art is the elaboratings of violence. Don't look to me to want to do anything about the world: I'm out of it."

"But if there hadn't been between you two the dark streets, the risks, and the old man you had just abandoned, in short had there been no danger, would you have hurried so eagerly?"

"**D**arling," Propertius says to Cynthia who isn't in front of him, "I know you've been going through hell because I've been refusing to speak to you.

"I know the minute I stopped talking to you, you'd slit your wrist (you did that just cause when you were in your teens you cut your arms with a razor blade regularly to teach yourself you were horror), then more seriously you obtained an ovarian infection because your ovaries had been rejected you tried I know you tried you did avoid me (except when you phoned my girlfriend answered the phone you hung up).

"Listen, Cynthia. I fucked so many girls, I took them up to this penthouse sauna and swimming pool someone lent me. Beautiful girls pass each other on the stairway. Limbs disappear in the shadow, and then there's nothing else.

I'm living with a girl. I don't even know her."

PROPERTIUS IS TELLING CYNTHIA WHO HIS CURRENT GIRLFRIEND IS. "The more I knew she was fucking the men she met through me behind my back, the more I'd do anything for her—crazed because I knew every move she made was planning to leave me. By allowing female emotions, I drive them away. Then it all stopped, she ran away with her other boyfriend.

"So I want you.

"If you're not obsessed for me, bitch, you're going to drink blood—you now living off your grandmother's capitalist hoard though blowing more—your food whatever you eat must always stink of rotten guts, human, always always you must regret everything you are. The thoughts that have to be imaginings must make you victim eat you, hole. You're looking everywhere you're looking everywhere you're looking everywhere you're looking everywhere: Every human is so stupid there're only ravenous wolves. Cats and dogs now gone wild are gnawing the crumbling white concrete blocks. Long red pointed finger-nails separate the cunt lip flesh, then digging into the soft purple, and around the protrusion of the nipple right there, another fingernail.

There are no more images. This is what it is, this is why you can't run from me. There's only obsession.

"Love will turn on the lover and gnaw."

Propertius is down on his knees because he's helpless.

"Last night I had a dream Cynthia. You were standing over me, the ring I had given you, your finger, your hand white palm outstretched. You said the following words to me:

'I didn't mean to tell your girlfriend was fuck-ing around but 1) you had just told me I wasn't a female because I have a 'career' and because I'm not a female no man will love me. That hurt. 2) You set up the terms of the relationship, but I was thinking about you all the time, so you said STAY RATIONAL at a time I wasn't rational: this was confusing me. I explained my identity-desperation by telling you I had known your girlfriend was two-timing you that was why I lov-ed you. But the second I just mentioned the first word, explosion!, so I backed off: I just heard gossip, the gossip was old she wasn't fucking anyone else. I'm wrong to listen to gossip. Let me be hurt. 3) I said 'Propertius is no more,' but my body reacted: I cut a razor blade through my flesh so I could see the flesh hole revealing two thin purple-blue-gray wires which frightened and reminded me of my mother's chin three days after she committed suicide, the body gets sick. I'm not a woman who takes shit, but

'Why do I like you so much? I like you so much you're necessary to the continuing of my existence right now and I don't understand this at all, I just know it's true.'

Cynthia walked away from me, and I woke up.''

PROPERTIUS TALKS TO CYNTHIA WHO ISN'T IN FRONT OF HIM. "I don't want you, slut, because love is mad and I don't want to be mad."

My mother committed suicide and I ran away. My mother committed suicide in a hotel room because she was lonely and there was no one else in the world but her, wants go so deep there is no way of getting them out of the body, no surgery other than death, the body will hurt. There are times when there is no food and those times must be sat through.

I ran away from pain.

What is, is. No fantasy. Pain. Just the details: the streets, the green garbage bag a bum's sleeping next to, a friend, too much time no time, too much to eat not enough to eat, going to a movie with Jeffrey I don't know if the world is better or worse than it has been I know the only anguish comes from running away.

Dear mother,

End